JUNIOR
NINJA
CHAMPION

By
Catherine Hapka

Houghton Mifflin Harcourt
BOSTON NEW YORK

hmhco.com

The text was set in Minion Pro.

Library of Congress Cataloging-in-Publication Data
Names: Hapka, Cathy, author.
Title: The fastest finish / by Catherine Hapka.
Description: Boston ; New York : Houghton Mifflin Harcourt, [2019] | Series: Junior ninja champion | Summary: The producers of *Junior Ninja Champion* announce a wildcard episode, throwing the team from Fit Kidz Gym off balance and forcing them to accept a new competitor on their team. Identifiers: LCCN 2018020062 | ISBN 9781328859013 (hardback) Subjects: | CYAC: Athletes—Fiction. | Friendship—Fiction. | Reality television programs—Fiction. | Contests—Fiction. | Competition (Psychology)—Fiction. | BISAC: JUVENILE FICTION / Sports & Recreation / Extreme Sports. | JUVENILE FICTION / Media Tie-In. | JUVENILE FICTION / Social Issues / Friendship. | JUVENILE FICTION / Action & Adventure / General.
Classification: LCC PZ7.H1996 Fas 2019 | DDC [Fic]—dc23
LC record available at https://lccn.loc.gov/2018020062

Printed in the United States of America
DOC 10 9 8 7 6 5 4 3 2 1
4500739468

Believe you can and you're halfway there.
— Theodore Roosevelt

JUNIOR
NINJA
CHAMPION

One

HURRY UP!" MACKENZIE CLARK exclaimed as she jumped out of the car. "We don't want to miss a second of the show!"

"Don't worry, we have plenty of time," Papa Kurt said.

"Yeah." Daddy Jim smiled and pushed his glasses up his nose. "Besides, we're recording it at home. You can watch every second of it as many times as you want."

"That's not the point." Mackenzie glanced from her fathers to the Fit Kidz gym. Every window was glowing in the fading evening light. "This is the premiere!"

It seemed to take forever, but finally her dads were out of the car and walking toward the entrance. Mackenzie rushed ahead, her long limbs quivering with excitement.

The big night was finally here! Tonight was the broadcast premiere of *Junior Ninja Champion* — and they were starting with her episode!

Most people who knew Mackenzie were still surprised that she'd decided to become a ninja. She was still a little surprised herself. She'd always been proud to be a nerd, more interested in science fiction than in sports. In fact, she'd always joked that she was allergic to exercise. But being a ninja — swinging around on bars or ropes, climbing up walls, jumping and balancing on all kinds of crazy obstacles — well, that didn't feel like exercise. It felt like fun!

The viewing party for the show was already in full swing when Mackenzie and her dads walked into the gym's big main room. It looked as if the entire town had turned out to celebrate. People of all ages crowded every corner. Mackenzie's science teacher was over by the refreshments table, and two of her neighbors were perched on a weight bench, sipping punch.

"Yo, Mack!" Ty Santiago yelled.

Mackenzie followed her teammate's voice. Ty was leaning against the spiral staircase that led up to the running track on the mezzanine. JJ Johnson was perched on one of the steps.

Mackenzie waved to the two boys, who were both on the Fit Kidz Junior Ninja team with her. She glanced around for Izzy Fitzgerald and Kevin Marshall, their other two teammates, but they were nowhere in sight.

"Go on and talk to your friends," Papa Kurt said with a smile. "We'll mingle."

Mackenzie didn't have to be told twice. She took off toward Ty and JJ.

JJ grinned when she reached them. "Can you believe we're about to be TV stars? Every single one of my cousins came tonight."

"My dads are here, too." Mackenzie waved a hand toward the spot where she'd left her fathers, though they'd already disappeared into the crowd. "It's too bad my birth mom is away on a business trip. But she promised to watch at her hotel."

"Cool." Ty pointed to several guys his age who had just entered. "Hey, check it out. It's my boys from the baseball team!"

He grinned and pumped a fist at the guys. Mackenzie smiled as the other guys whooped and waved back. Ty was the opposite of Mackenzie in many ways. He was superathletic and seemed to be great at just about every sport there was. His parents owned the gym where the ninja team trained.

Then there was JJ. He wasn't into team sports the way Ty was, but he loved climbing around in the huge tree house he and his dad had built in their backyard, which meant he was a natural at being a ninja. When Mackenzie glanced at him now, JJ was waving to someone in the opposite direction from Ty's friends — a petite woman with dark hair and a tattoo of a firecracker on her bicep. She was chatting with Ty's parents next to the far windows.

"Hey, Tara's here!" Mackenzie exclaimed when she saw the woman. Tara "Tiny Torpedo" Warner was the coach of the team. She was also a ninja herself—she'd appeared on *National Ninja Champion,* the adult version of *JNC.*

"Of course she's here," JJ said with a laugh. "There's no way she'd miss this!"

Just then a portly man with a handlebar mustache hurried into the room. Next to him was a young kid wearing a cape and alien antennas on his head. They both waved at Mackenzie as they headed over toward the refreshments table.

"Friends of yours?" JJ asked.

"Yeah," Mackenzie said. "That's Carl—he owns the comic book store over on Oak Street. He told me his son is a huge ninja fan. I can't believe how many people turned out to watch! Look, here come the others."

Izzy and Kevin were weaving toward them through the crowd. Izzy was sipping from a paper cup. As usual, Mackenzie thought, she looked supercool in her leather jacket and high-top sneakers, the purple streak in her hair making her look sort of like an anime character. Kevin, a few inches shorter than Izzy, had his black curly hair buzzed short and was wearing khaki shorts and a plain blue T-shirt.

"Hey, it's the odd couple," Ty joked when they arrived.

Izzy frowned. "Who are you calling odd, weirdo?"

Ty held up both hands. "Chill, it was just a joke," he said. "You know — because you're tall and Kev's short?"

Izzy rolled her eyes, but Kevin just laughed. "I'm glad you finally got here, Mackenzie," he said.

"Me, too. Daddy Jim got a phone call right when we were leaving." Mackenzie glanced at Izzy's cup. "I think I'll get some punch before the show starts."

Halfway to the punch bowl, Mackenzie spotted another familiar face. "Hi, Noah," she said, veering off toward a slender dark-haired boy sitting on a leg press in the corner. "I didn't know you were coming."

Noah Dhawan glanced up from poking at a half-eaten cookie on a paper plate. "I didn't either," he said with a shy but friendly smile. "My mom heard about it from your dad, and she said we should go."

Noah's mother, Stella Perry-Dhawan, directed most of the shows for the local community theater. Daddy Jim had acted in a few shows, including a recent production of *Fiddler on the Roof*.

Noah himself was a talented dancer and had appeared in most of his mom's shows. He never seemed to have a speaking or singing part, but he was always one of the best dancers on the stage.

"Did you see my review of *Fiddler* on the blog?"

Mackenzie asked him. "I mentioned how great you were in your scenes."

Her blog, *Mack Attacks,* covered lots of topics—pretty much anything that interested her, which was almost everything. Lately she'd mostly been writing about *Junior Ninja Champion,* but a few days earlier she'd written a long review of the play, which had been great. Daddy Jim had played the village rabbi, and Noah had been one of the Russian dancers. He'd been much better than the other Russian dancers, though Mackenzie hadn't mentioned that in the blog.

"Uh-huh, I saw it. Thanks." Noah flashed her another brief smile. Then he went back to poking at his cookie.

Mackenzie waited a second to see if he would say anything else. But he didn't. That was typical. Noah seemed superconfident when he was dancing onstage, but he was pretty shy the rest of the time. Mackenzie felt as if she barely knew anything about him, even though she'd known him for years—and even though her dads liked to joke that she was so outgoing that she could make friends with a tree!

Across the room, a loud laugh rang out. Noah's mom was over there, talking to a big group of people.

Too bad some of his mom's friendliness didn't rub off on Noah, Mackenzie thought.

Just then she heard a loud whistle. Ty's parents were standing on the little stage they'd set up at one end of the gym. Mrs. Santiago was fiddling with a big-screen TV while Mr. Santiago was calling for attention.

"Ready, everyone?" Ty's dad called out with a grin. "Find a seat — the show's about to start!"

Two

ALL FIVE TEAM MEMBERS were sitting together right up front with Coach Tara. JJ held his breath as the TV came on. It was showing a car commercial, but the show was due to begin at any moment. When Ty elbowed him in the ribs, JJ let out the breath he was holding.

"Dude," Ty whispered. "Can you believe we're about to be on TV?"

"No," JJ whispered back.

That was the truth. JJ considered himself a pretty ordinary kid. He'd never been interested in being famous or having everyone look at him. Or about winning or being the best. He'd always left that sort of thing to his older sister, Jasmine. JJ had been happy just to hang out in his backyard tree house with his friends and do other normal stuff like that.

He turned and scanned the crowd in the darkened gym. Finally he spotted his family—his parents, his aunts and uncles, and all twelve cousins. Jasmine was right at the front of the group. She waved when she saw him looking. JJ was still a little surprised that she was there. Normally she never missed her Thursday-night choir practice.

"Look—it's on!" Mackenzie squealed loudly.

JJ quickly waved to his sister and then turned back to the TV screen. The *Junior Ninja Champion* logo had just appeared, and exciting music was playing. JJ shivered.

"This is it!" he said.

But nobody heard him, because everyone was cheering loudly. The crowd in the gym quieted down when a tall, athletic-looking woman appeared on camera. She was standing in front of a huge obstacle course. JJ knew it was the same one where he and his friends had competed, but it looked even more impressive on TV.

"Welcome to the very first episode of *Junior Ninja Champion*!" the woman said, grinning widely into the camera. "I'm Mellie Monroe, and I'll be your host for all six exciting episodes—and the even more exciting finals!"

Mellie went on to explain how the show would work. Each week it would feature a semifinals competition from a different part of the country, showing lots of kids trying to make it through a challenging course of obstacles that tested their strength, balance, and agility. At the end of each episode the audience would learn which ninjas had made the finals.

"But we already know, right?" Kevin whispered to JJ.

JJ grinned and gave Kevin a thumbs-up. "Only for our episode, though," he whispered back. "We'll have to wait to see who makes the finals from the other shows."

The Fit Kidz ninjas had signed some legal papers promising not to tell anyone the results of their show. So had the competitors from the other five semifinals. JJ knew that some of his friends wished they knew all the results already, but he liked the suspense of waiting to find out what had happened on the other shows.

The host was still talking, explaining the rules. Only ninjas between the ages of nine and thirteen could compete. No ninja was allowed to try the course before the competition. That sort of thing.

But JJ already knew all that stuff. He tapped his foot impatiently, eager for the action to start. All of Mellie's explanations reminded him of the credits that played at the beginning of his favorite video game. He always counted the seconds until that was over, too.

Mellie finally stopped talking, and the camera shifted to the first ninja, a dark-haired girl. As she stood on the mat at the beginning of the course, her "package" started to play. That was what the show's producers called the short film that played before each ninja's round. The package gave the ninja's name and age, their nickname if they had one, and a few other interesting things about him or her. In this case, the dark-haired girl talked about how doing agility competitions with her dog had inspired her to become a ninja.

Then the girl started her course. JJ remembered her—she'd wiped out on the fourth obstacle. But he didn't say anything about that out loud. He didn't want to spoil it for anyone who hadn't been there.

After that, the next two ninjas took their turns, though neither of them did much better than the first one. Then came a commercial break. JJ sat back as an ad for a new movie started to play.

"Wow, this is cool," he told his teammates. "It's so exciting that I almost forget I already know what happens."

Izzy nodded and bumped Kevin's shoulder with hers. "You were the next one to go," she reminded him.

JJ realized that Izzy was right. Kevin had been the fourth ninja to attack the course—and the first from Fit Kidz.

"Oh my gosh, this is so exciting!" Mackenzie exclaimed. She leaped to her feet and did a little happy dance, which made them all laugh.

When the show returned and everyone saw Kevin standing on the mat, the room erupted in cheers. Ty stood and pulled Kevin up beside him.

"Take a bow, bro," he urged with a grin.

Kevin waved and bowed to the crowd. JJ heard a loud whistle.

"Was that your mom?" JJ exclaimed in surprise. Mrs. Marshall hardly ever smiled, and she had lots of strict rules that Kevin and his younger brother, Darius, were expected to follow at all times. Especially Kevin, since he'd had cancer when he was younger and his mom was scared to let him do anything that might get him hurt. She almost hadn't let him be a ninja at all. She definitely didn't seem like the type of person who could whistle like that!

"Probably." Kevin laughed. "Usually she only whistles to call Darius and me in for dinner."

Then they all stopped talking, because Kevin's package was playing. It started off by describing how he'd beaten cancer a few years earlier. Many of the people in the room already knew about that, but JJ could hear gasps from others, and one woman exclaimed "Poor baby!" so loudly that everyone could hear her. When Mrs. Marshall spoke about how proud she was of Kevin, JJ could hear sniffles from all around the room.

He glanced at Kevin, who looked kind of embarrassed. But then JJ forgot about that because the package was ending and Kevin was starting his course.

JJ leaned forward, watching as his friend leaped up and grabbed the rings of the first obstacle, which was called the Ring-a-Ding Swing. He cheered along with everyone else when Kevin swung himself along from ring to ring and landed on the mat at the end, barely pausing to rest before leaping forward onto the first of the five balance steps known as Stepping Out.

JJ's foot twitched, almost as if he were doing the obstacle himself. *Jump forward, hit the middle of the block, push off* . . . He'd worked hard to master the balance obstacles, which hadn't come as easily to him as the climbing and swinging ones. Onscreen, Kevin skipped through the blocks, making it look easy.

Even though JJ already knew what was going to happen, he groaned when Kevin's hand slipped on the fifth obstacle, the tire swing, sending him tumbling down into the safety net. Everyone else in the room groaned, too — even Kevin himself! But when the Kevin on TV climbed out of the net and gave everyone a thumbs-up, the room erupted in cheers once again.

The rest of the episode seemed to fly by. Mackenzie was the next Fit Kidz competitor to go. She let out a whoop when she appeared on the mat, which made JJ and everybody else laugh. When she fell on the sixth obstacle, most of the people in the gym groaned. But when JJ glanced over at Mackenzie, she was beaming at the TV set, looking happy and proud of herself.

Ty had a much different reaction to his appearance. He'd made it through the entire course, but had just missed at the Crazy Cliff. Everyone cheered anyway, but Ty looked as if he wanted to crawl under his chair and never come out.

After that it was Izzy's turn. When she flew up the Crazy Cliff, the tall, steep, curved wall that was the final obstacle on the course, the crowd in the gym went wild. Izzy looked a little embarrassed, and she rolled her eyes when Mackenzie grabbed her arm and dragged her to her feet. But JJ grinned and joined in as Mackenzie led the whole team — including Izzy — in a happy dance.

Finally it was JJ's turn. It felt strange to see his own familiar face appear on TV.

"Weird," he commented as he watched himself step onto the mat. "I was really nervous, but you can't tell."

"Nope. You mostly just look really focused," Ty said. "Here's your package."

JJ had been so nervous at the show that he hadn't paid much attention to his package. But he watched it now. It showed him climbing around in the tree house he and his dad had built and playing kickball with his friends and cousins. There was even a shot of him roller-skating with Jasmine.

Then the package was over, and JJ was starting the course. He felt nervous all over again as he watched himself leap up to grab the first ring, even though he knew he'd made it through the Ring-a-Ding Swing easily. Next came the balance steps, which had been a lot harder. He'd slipped on the last step, almost losing his balance. A gasp went up from the crowd as he flung himself forward, barely making it onto the mat.

The next few obstacles passed in a flash. Finally the JJ on TV stood looking up at the Crazy Cliff—probably the most famous obstacle on the show. Now, in the Fit Kidz gym, JJ's heart pounded with excitement. This was better than the best video game he'd ever played. It was almost as fun watching himself do the course as it had been to do it!

"Climb that cliff! Climb that cliff!" the audience in the gym chanted, almost drowning out the audience on the show, which was chanting the same thing.

"Climb that cliff!" JJ cried as he saw himself starting to run . . .

A huge cheer rang out when JJ made it to the top and leaped to his feet. His teammates cheered louder than anyone, even though they already knew what had happened.

"Take a bow, ninja!" Izzy said, giving JJ a shove.

JJ jumped to his feet and waved, which brought even louder cheers. It was weird being the center of attention. After all, he was just an ordinary kid. But maybe it was okay being a little more than ordinary for once. Maybe it was even kind of fun!

Three

WAY TO GO, TY!" Coach Channing slapped Ty on the back. "You looked strong out there, son."

"Thanks, Coach." Ty forced a grin for his school basketball coach, but he felt a little weird. Watching the show had been fun. But it also reminded him that he'd failed. Unlike JJ and Izzy, he hadn't completed the course. He'd made it all the way through and then wiped out on the Crazy Cliff. Because of that, he hadn't made the finals, at least not for sure—he was only an alternate. That was better than Kevin and Mackenzie, who hadn't made it at all. But if you weren't a winner, you were a loser—everyone knew that. And Ty hated feeling like a loser.

The coach wandered off, and more people came over

to talk to Ty—some of his friends from the baseball team, his dentist, people from the gym, neighbors. All of them seemed to think that he'd done great.

But Ty knew better. *If only I'd pushed a little harder, made it up that cliff,* he told himself for the zillionth time since the competition. *Then I'd still be on track to become the first-ever Junior Ninja champion . . .*

"Santiago—" A familiar voice snapped him out of his gloomy thoughts.

"Coach Driscoll!" Ty gulped, suddenly a little nervous to face his soccer coach. Ty had skipped tryouts for the coach's local travel league to be on *JNC*. Was he mad? Especially since Ty hadn't even made the finals?

But the coach was smiling. "It's not every day one of my players is on national TV. Congrats."

"Um, thanks." Ty wasn't sure what else to say. "Kinda wish I'd made the finals, though." He shot the coach a sidelong glance. "Especially since I missed soccer tryouts to do it."

Coach Driscoll scratched his beard, looking thoughtful. "Did you have fun?"

"You mean being a ninja? Sure, it was a blast!" Ty grinned. "One of the funnest things I've ever done." His smile faded. "But now I'm going to miss a whole season of travel soccer." He shrugged. "I thought, uh, you might be bummed about that."

The coach smiled. "Life is about choices, Santiago.

You chose ninja-ing over soccer this time. That's cool with me."

"Really?" Ty was surprised. Coach Driscoll took soccer really seriously. He'd helped Ty become a much better player.

"Really," the coach said. "Listen, did I ever tell you that all three of my older brothers were basketball stars back in school?"

"I don't think so."

"Well, they were. So it was practically a family rebellion when I decided I liked soccer better." Coach Driscoll grinned. "My oldest brother wanted to disown me. But my parents said it was up to me. You gotta do what you love — you only live once. That's what they said. And that's what I'm saying to you now." He patted Ty on the shoulder. "If you want to be a ninja, be a ninja. But don't second-guess yourself. That'll just make you crazy."

Ty nodded slowly. "I get it, I guess. Thanks, Coach."

The finals taping in Hollywood was less than two months away. That meant there was no time to waste! The next morning, the team met at the gym to get back to work. JJ and Kevin were already in the ninja room when Ty walked in. JJ was scrambling up the climbing wall while Kevin practiced on the balance steps. Both of them were smiling and looking as if they were having a blast.

Coach Tara was there, too. "Morning, Ty," she said

cheerfully. "I hope being a TV star hasn't gone to your head too much. Because it's time to get back to business. We've got a finals show to train for!"

You mean Iz and JJ have a finals show to train for, Ty thought.

But he didn't say it, flashing back to Coach Driscoll's words: *Don't second-guess yourself.*

"I'm ready," he told Tara instead, flexing his muscles.

As he started his warm-up, Ty glanced over at JJ again. He'd been an alternate after tryouts and had ended up being on the show—and finishing the course. Maybe the same thing would happen to Ty!

All I need is a chance to get on that finals show, he thought as he did a few lunges and stretches. *Then it's up to me to do the rest. And this time I won't choke!*

Soon Izzy arrived and started her warm-up. Tara glanced at her watch.

"Where's Mackenzie?" she asked. "Well, she'll just have to catch up when she gets here. We have a lot to do today!" She clapped her hands. "Okay, team—five laps around the room, and don't dawdle! Let's get that blood pumping!"

Ty fell into step with the others. He was used to running laps, since most of his coaches used running to build wind. But he was itching to move on to the ninja obstacles.

"Faster!" Tara shouted. "I want to see a team of ninjas, not a bunch of turtles!"

"I thought you might take it easy on us today," Izzy

called to Tara with a grin. "We were up late watching ourselves on TV, remember?"

"Tough," Tara retorted, laughing. "Now move those legs! Hup, hup!"

"Being a ninja TV star isn't as glamorous as I thought," Ty joked.

Tara laughed again. "You're right about that." Then she glanced at the door. "Well, well—look who finally decided to show up."

It was Mackenzie, looking wide-eyed and excited. Then again, she almost always looked that way. Still, something about the way she was waving her arms around made Ty slow down and watch her.

"Hey guys, guess what!" Mackenzie cried. "The overnights are in, and it's official—*Junior Ninja Champion* is a huge hit!"

KEVIN RUSHED OVER to Mackenzie, along with the rest of the group.

"What are overnights?" JJ asked.

"It's a hit?" Izzy added. "Really?"

Kevin waited to hear what Mackenzie would say. Somehow she always seemed to know how stuff worked. Probably because she spent a lot of time online. Her dads trusted her a lot, so her computer time wasn't limited the way Kevin's — or most of the others — was.

"Overnights is just another word for TV ratings." Mackenzie flopped onto a pile of spare mats to catch her breath. "And the ratings show that *JNC* is already doing great with viewers all over the country, even after just one show."

"Ours," Ty put in, puffing out his chest proudly.

"Right." Mackenzie grinned. "Actually it looks like it's going to be just as popular as *National Ninja Champion*!"

"Wow," Kevin said. "That's one of the top shows on TV!"

"That's great," Tara said. "Sounds like you guys are even bigger stars than you thought." She winked and clapped her hands. "Now let's get back to work."

After practice, it took Kevin only ten minutes to walk from the gym to his neighborhood in the oldest part of town. His street was lined with beautiful historic houses and huge old trees that shaded the street. The only bad thing about living there was that the yards were really small. Most kids played at the park or in the empty lot at the end of Kevin's block.

Today he heard shouts and laughter coming from the lot as he approached. He glanced over and saw the Nguyen twins playing kickball with six or seven of their friends.

Kevin kept walking. The Nguyens were thirteen, two years older than he was, so he didn't know them that well.

"Yo, Kevin! Kevin Marshall, hold up!"

Kevin stopped, surprised. When he turned, Gabe Nguyen was loping toward him, followed by his brother. The other kids were right behind them.

"Check it out," one of the kids said. "It's the neighborhood TV star!"

Eric Nguyen grinned at Kevin. "We saw your show last night," he said. "It was totally cool!"

"Um, thanks. It was no big deal." These kids were treating Kevin as if he were some kind of celebrity, and he wasn't sure he liked it. It didn't feel right.

"No big deal?" A tall girl — Kevin was pretty sure her name was Olivia — laughed and gave him a playful smack on the shoulder. "Don't be modest, Kevin. You're a ninja superstar!"

"Yeah," another kid said. "Better get used to the attention."

Better get used to the attention. Something about those words seemed familiar. But why?

Suddenly Kevin got it. His doctor had told him something like that back when he was sick. Having cancer had made him the center of attention, too. Everyone had always wanted to know how he was doing, if the treatments were working, stuff like that. The doctors explained that it was normal — people cared and wanted to make him feel better. But Kevin had hated it.

He jerked out of his memories when Gabe poked him in the arm. "Want to join the game?" Gabe asked. "My team's one short, and I could use a good athlete like you."

"No fair!" a girl with cornrows protested. "I want to be on Kevin's team."

Olivia grinned and held up the ball. "Tough," she said. "He's with us. Right, Kev?"

Kevin shrugged, still a little surprised that the older kids were paying so much attention to him. “Sure,” he said.

“Cool.” Olivia tossed him the ball.

Kevin drop-kicked it, sending it flying back into the empty lot. Then he jogged after it.

He’d definitely hated being a cancer celebrity. But so far, being a ninja celebrity was turning out to be a lot more fun!

Five

IZZY KICKED OFF at the top of the Polk Street hill, then glided down on her skateboard. It was a hot day, and the breeze felt good. She was running a little late, since her stepmonster, Tina, had insisted that Izzy unload the dishwasher before she left for the gym.

At the bottom of the hill, she shifted her weight to curve left onto Ninth Street. Halfway down the block she spotted a lone figure skateboarding in the parking lot by the gas station.

Izzy skidded to a stop. "Jess!" she blurted out.

Her mind spun as her friend jumped a curb and then turned to face her, kicking her skateboard end-up into her hand. "Iz, what's up," Jess said casually.

"I was just going to ask you that." Izzy couldn't believe that Jess was right here in front of her. She hadn't heard from her in weeks! "Where've you been? Did you get my text about the premiere party?"

Jess shrugged, squinting up toward the sky. "Couldn't make it. I was busy."

Izzy's head spun. Why was Jess acting so weird? Like they weren't even friends. Yeah, she was older and cooler than Izzy, but that had never seemed to come between them before.

"Busy?" Izzy tried to turn it into a joke. "Come on, Jess. You're the whole reason I ended up on that show in the first place."

It was true. Jess and Izzy had been skateboarding in the parking lot of a local shopping center when Jess dared Izzy to ride down a steep stairwell. Izzy hadn't wanted to do it, as she was a tiny bit scared of heights. But she never turned down a challenge, especially in front of Jess. She'd panicked halfway down, and her skateboard had ended up getting away from her and crashing through a restaurant window. As punishment, her parents had sent her to run laps at Fit Kidz every day after school, and the rest was history.

"Don't blame me for that," Jess snapped. "You're the one who blew it, not me." She dropped her board, jumping on and setting it rolling in one smooth move. "Gotta bounce," she muttered.

She whizzed past before Izzy could say another word,

disappearing around the corner seconds later. Izzy just stood there, confused and hurt. She hadn't seen or heard from Jess since that night at the shopping center. But that hadn't seemed too strange—Izzy had been stuck at the gym every day, and then the ninja thing happened and kept her even busier. Plus her parents had taken away her phone after the window-breaking incident, and they'd given it back only a week or two earlier.

But maybe there was another reason she hadn't heard from her friend. Had Jess actually been avoiding her all this time? Why?

Izzy was still feeling distracted when she got to the gym. Ty, JJ, and Kevin were already in the ninja room warming up, though Mackenzie was nowhere in sight. When Izzy walked in, the three boys were talking about the trip to Los Angeles for the finals.

". . . and my mom talked to your parents, and it's all arranged," Kevin was saying. "I still can't believe she's going to let me go all the way out to California without her!"

"Cool." JJ smiled. "Hi, Izzy. Did you hear that? The three of us get to share a hotel room." He hooked a thumb at the other two boys. "Maybe you and Mackenzie should try to bunk together."

"Maybe," Izzy muttered, not particularly interested. Still, she was happy to hear that Kevin was definitely going to the finals. They'd all been afraid that his mom wouldn't let him make the trip to Los Angeles, since he wouldn't be competing. But his mom had agreed to fly him out there as an early birthday gift, even though she couldn't go herself because of work.

The rest of the families would be there, though — even Izzy's. That had been a surprise. She knew they'd have to miss out on their town's annual Labor Day half marathon. And the Fitzgeralds were runners. That's what her dad always said. Besides that, her brother, Charlie, had won his age group last year, so he was giving up the chance to defend his title. Izzy still couldn't quite believe he was willing to do that.

Just then Tara strode in. "Look alive, ninjas!" she said. "Let's get moving."

Izzy tried to focus on warming up with the rest of the team, but she couldn't stop thinking about Jess. What was her problem, anyway?

"Alternating lunges, people!" Tara ordered. "Keep going until I say stop."

Izzy obeyed, doing lunges alongside the others. But her mind was still on her friend. Or *was* Jess her friend? Izzy had always wondered why the older girl wanted to hang out with her. Sure, both of them were into skateboarding and parkour. But maybe that wasn't enough. Maybe Jess had decided that hanging out with a twelve-year-old was boring . . .

"Izzy, heads up!" Kevin said. "We're supposed to do pull-ups now!"

Izzy snapped out of her thoughts. The others were scrambling toward the pull-up bars while she was still in mid-lunge. "Sorry," she muttered.

"Mind in the game, Iz," Tara said. "Being a good ninja is mental, not just physical."

"I know, I know." Izzy jumped up and grabbed a free bar, grunting as she did her first pull-up. Exercises like this, which relied almost totally on upper body strength, were a lot harder for her than the balance or agility stuff, so for the next few minutes she didn't have much energy to spare worrying about Jess.

Tara had just ordered them all to move on to the climbing wall when Mackenzie rushed in, pink-cheeked and out of breath.

"Sorry I'm late again!" she cried. "But you'll forgive me when you hear the huge news."

"What is—" Ty began.

But Mackenzie didn't even let him finish. "There's going to be a wildcard show!" she exclaimed, clapping her hands. "Isn't that amazing?"

"A what?" Izzy said. She had no idea what Mackenzie was talking about.

"What's a wildcard show?" JJ added.

"It's like an extra show—*JNC* is such a huge success that they want even more kids to be a part of it," Mackenzie said. "It works like this . . ."

Six

MACK ATTACKS . . . . . .

MY BLOG ABOUT INTERESTING STUFF

By Mackenzie Clark, age 10½, nerdgirl extraordinaire! (← *that last word means fab!*)

Today: MACK ATTACKS . . . . . . Wildcard Ninjas!!!

Big news, loyal readers! So I already posted what a big hit *JNC* is. But I just found out something even **more** amazing. The producers want to make the finals even **bigger and better**. So they just announced that they're adding a wildcard show!!!

What's a wildcard show, you ask? Well, I'm going to tell you! It works like this:

1. In two weeks, there will be another day of tryouts in all the same locations as last time — which means one of them is right down the road in North Creek again, where my teammates and I tried out.
2. The course will be different from last time, since the producers assume some of the same people will try out again. (Though nobody who actually made the semis is allowed to try again even if they didn't make the finals — they want to give new people a chance.)
3. A bunch of ninjas will make it through to the wildcard show. It's going to be a little different from our semis shows, since it will tape at all six semifinals locations, but the show's editors will combine it all into one show. Complicated, right? But that way all the wildcard ninjas from across the country can compete against each other — the courses will be identical in all the locations, and Mellie Monroe can still host them all, thanks to the wonders of technology, ha ha!
4. They're expecting tons of people to try out this time, since the show is way more famous now — everyone is watching!
5. The best ten finishers from the wildcard show will advance to the finals competition on Labor Day

weekend — just like the top ten ninjas from each of the original semifinals shows. **EXCEPT** . . .

6. . . . if there aren't ten wildcard ninjas who score better than the lowest-scoring finalists from the original semis, then the alternates from those shows get called back for the finals instead. (Which means my friend Ty still has a great shot at competing! Whoo!)
7. So that makes the finals even bigger and better and more awesome!!!! I can't WAIT to see what happens!

Seven

"IT'S NOT FAIR," Ty muttered, glaring down at the cereal floating in his bowl.

His mother glanced up from her coffee and sighed. "Ty . . ."

"No, I mean it." He shifted his glare to his parents, who were both watching him now. "I know you said I should stop griping about this. But seriously, who came up with such a stupid plan?"

"The producers of the show," his father said from over by the stove, where he was making eggs. "And clearly they don't think it's stupid."

"Well, they're wrong." Ty scowled. "I should have a shot

at one of those wildcard spots! I'm probably a better ninja than anyone who'll try out this time."

His mom shrugged. "That may or may not be true, but it's not the point."

"Then what is the point?" Ty shoved his bowl away, sloshing milk on the table, but not caring. "I should be on that finals show, not some newbie!"

"We talked about this last night," Ty's dad said. "We can't read the producers' minds, but there are plenty of reasons why they might have decided to set it up this way." He ticked them off on his fingers. "One, they want to give more kids a chance to compete. Two, it's a way to pump up the drama—everyone will want to find out whether ten new ninjas will beat the alternates."

Ty's mother nodded. "TV's all about the ratings."

"Now you sound like Mackenzie," Ty muttered. She'd said pretty much the same thing when she told them about the wildcard stuff yesterday. But it still didn't make sense to Ty.

"Chin up, Ty, and stop complaining," his dad said. "You're still an alternate. That puts you a step ahead of some of your teammates. They can't try out for the wildcard, either, which means they have no shot at the finals."

"Yeah, but they don't care that much." Ty shook his head. Mackenzie and Kevin both actually seemed excited about the whole wildcard thing. He didn't get it. "Anyway, it's not fair."

"Since when is life fair?" His mother shrugged. "All you can do is your best, and see what happens."

"Whatever," Ty grumbled. He knew his parents were right. Maybe he'd luck out; maybe he'd get called in as an alternate, just like JJ. But he hated having something like that be totally out of his control.

Ty was still in a bad mood when that day's training session began. After their warm-up, Tara decided to start on the structure the kids called the Climbing Thing. It was a sturdy metal frame with lots of bars, ropes, and rings hanging from it.

"Try to get across from this corner to that one," she announced, pointing out a diagonal path. "No legs allowed, just arms. Who wants to try first?"

"I will," Mackenzie said with a laugh. "Because there's no way I can do that."

"Be positive," Tara chided her.

Mackenzie grinned. "Okay, I'm *positive* I can't do that!"

Everyone laughed, even Tara. Then the coach told Mackenzie to go ahead.

Mackenzie was right — she didn't make it all the way across. But she seemed surprised and happy that she managed to get more than halfway.

"I'll go next," Ty said. Working up a sweat always made him feel better, and he needed to take his mind off this whole stupid wildcard thing.

At Tara's nod, Ty jumped up and grabbed the set of rings near the starting corner. He swung his legs, gaining momentum until he could reach out one arm and grab a knotted rope. The swing from that carried him easily to the swinging bar.

Then came a tire swing, and after that a cargo net . . . Ty's muscles were burning by then, but it felt good. He felt strong — like a real ninja.

Next came the hardest part of the challenge — a fixed bar that was too far away to grab without letting go of the net. That meant Ty had to gather his strength and jump for it.

"Aaah!" he cried as his right hand missed the bar. His left hand grabbed it, but he felt his grip slipping . . .

But somehow he held on until he could get his right hand around the bar. Whew! That had been close. Ty was vaguely aware of his friends cheering, but he was already focused on the next step, another set of rings. He got there and then swung over to the first of a set of hanging balls. Two more balls, and he was across!

"That was awesome, Ty!" Mackenzie cried as the rest of the team cheered.

Tara smiled. "That's how you do it," she agreed, stepping over to give him a fist bump. "JJ? Want to go next?"

Ty leaned against the wall and caught his breath while he watched his teammate start the challenge. JJ was usually great at this sort of thing. He had an amazing tree house in his backyard, just a few doors down from Ty's house. It spanned several large oaks and maples, with multiple floors and lots of ropes and ladders and stuff to get around. JJ had even installed a bunch of climbing holds in the trunk of the main tree.

Sure enough, JJ made it past the halfway point easily. But when he tried to make the jump to the fixed bar, he wasn't even close.

"Oops," he said with a smile as he climbed to his feet on the mat beneath the bar.

Ty frowned. Why didn't JJ look more upset about messing up like that? He was a finalist—he should be taking this seriously!

But Tara didn't seem that upset, either. "Good try," she told JJ. Then she told Izzy to take her turn.

Izzy didn't even make it to the fixed bar. She lost her grip on the tire swing.

Once again, Ty felt annoyed. *I did the best, but they're the finalists. How is that fair?* he thought.

Kevin had just fallen near the middle of the Climbing Thing when the door opened. A skinny Indian kid stepped in and looked around.

"Is this where the ninja team trains?" he asked in a soft, uncertain voice.

"Uh-huh," Ty said, looking him over, wondering why he seemed kind of familiar.

"Noah!" Mackenzie exclaimed. "What are you doing here?"

Oh, right, Noah. Now Ty remembered. Mackenzie had pointed him out to them at the premiere party, though he couldn't remember what she'd said about him.

"Yes, this is the ninja room," Tara told Noah with a smile. "How can we help you?"

Noah took another step into the room and cleared his throat. "Um, I want to join the team," he said. "I'm going to try out for that wildcard show."

Eight

AFTER HIS ANNOUNCEMENT, Noah forced himself to stand up straight and face the ninja team. That tall, muscular kid — the owners' son, Ty — looked shocked.

"Are you serious?" Ty blurted out.

The others mostly looked surprised, too. Noah glanced from one face to the other. He knew their names from seeing them on TV, but the only ones he knew in person were the two girls. Well, really he only knew Mackenzie. Izzy Fitzgerald went to the same private school he did, but she was a year ahead of him.

"That's amazing!" Mackenzie shrieked, rushing forward. "Noah, you'll have so much fun! Right, guys?"

"Um, sure thing," JJ said.

Kevin and Izzy nodded. So did Tara.

"Welcome," she said, looking him up and down. "Noah, is it? Do you have any experience with ninja type skills?"

"Not really, no," Noah said.

"But he's an awesome dancer," Mackenzie spoke up again. "He does it all — contemporary, jazz, hip-hop, and, um, lots of other styles, I think. Right, Noah?"

"A dancer?" Ty sounded dubious. "This is a ninja team, not a ballet or whatever."

"Dancers are athletes, too," Noah said, a little annoyed by the older guy's attitude. Everyone in town knew that Ty was pretty much the star of every sports team there was. But Noah guessed he'd still have trouble executing a proper arabesque, never mind a cabriole or a grand jeté.

"That's true," Tara said, smiling. "A well-trained dancer is halfway to being a good ninja. Which is a good thing, since those tryouts are coming up fast."

"Yeah. You won't have much time to get ready," Ty put in, still sounding kind of aggressive.

Tara shot him a perplexed look. "Come on in, Noah, and let's see some of your moves so we can plan your training. Do you have a permission form from your parents?"

"I just dropped it off at the office." That was true, though Noah's parents didn't know the real reason he'd wanted to join Fit Kidz. They thought he was just there to stay in shape for his next set of auditions. Just cross-training — like throwing in a few ballroom or hip-hop classes to keep his dancing sharp.

Ty crossed his arms over his chest. "This won't take long, will it?" he said. "Because I thought the rest of us were supposed to be training. We have a show to get ready for, remember? Which means we don't have time to waste on some newbie."

"Ty, that's enough." Tara sounded annoyed. "One thing we definitely don't have time for here is rudeness. What happened to your team spirit?"

"I have plenty of team spirit — but only for the real team." Ty glared at her, looking sulky.

Tara shook her head and sighed, but didn't say anything else. She turned to Noah, who was feeling more and more uncomfortable — almost as uncomfortable as the time a couple of years ago when his mom had insisted he try out for the lead in *Oliver.* Maybe this whole ninja thing wasn't the best idea . . .

"Let's see what you've got, Noah," Tara said cheerfully. She pointed at a set of wooden blocks in the middle of the room. "See what you can do with the balance steps — you've seen the show, right? You know how they work?"

"Uh-huh." Noah didn't tell her that he'd seen *National Ninja Champion* only a handful of times. Normally he had dance classes in the evening, so he didn't have much spare time for TV. But after the premiere party he'd read everything he could find about it on the Internet. And seeing the show the other night was still fresh in his mind — he was sure he could copy what he'd seen. Figuring out how to get through these obstacles had to be easier than remembering choreography.

"Okay. If you make it through the steps, move on to the climbing wall, try the balance log, and then maybe the hanging rings," Tara said. "If you're still feeling good, you could finish with the Loco Ladder. Go!"

Noah nodded. Everyone was staring at him, but he tried not to let that shake him. *This is just like being onstage,* he told himself, shaking out his legs as he walked toward the steps. *Time to perform.*

The balance steps were five large, sloped blocks of wood set a few feet apart in two staggered rows. Noah knew from watching *JNC* that he was supposed to leap from one block to another — and that a lot of people had trouble keeping their balance through the whole set. But years of dancing had given him a good sense of balance and timing, and he made it through easily, landing lightly on the mat at the far end of the steps.

"Whoo! Go, Noah!" Mackenzie cheered.

Noah glanced over at her and smiled, then returned his attention to the course. He flexed his hands as he looked up at the climbing wall. Colorful holds were dotted all the way up. His arms were strong, but could he hang on to those tiny blocks of plastic?

He didn't stop to worry about it. Behind him, he could hear Ty muttering something to one of the others. But Noah was focused now, the way he always was onstage. Only this wall and his body existed, and he was going to perform.

His hand slipped once halfway up, and his heart pounded as he imagined himself falling. But somehow he flung his foot up and found the next hold. And then he was at the top!

He could hear Mackenzie cheering again as he slid down the rope that hung beside the wall. "Good job!" Tara called. "Balance log next."

"If you're not too tired, that is," Ty added.

Noah almost smiled. He wasn't even close to tired!

The balance log looked tricky. It was basically just what its name described—a huge log hanging horizontally on a metal pole, sort of like a balance beam except that it was free to rotate in either direction with the slightest shift in weight.

Noah took a few deep breaths, studying the log. Then he vaulted onto it, throwing out his arms to keep his balance as he felt it tip to the left.

"Easy, Noah!" Mackenzie called. "It's tricky!"

But it wasn't, not really. As soon as Noah found his balance point, he was able to walk perfectly straight, controlling his weight and posture just as he'd been trained to do in his earliest ballet classes.

This time he heard several cheers as he hopped off at

the far end of the obstacle, but he didn't look around to see who it was. The hanging rings were next. It was harder than he'd expected to swing far enough to grab the next ring, but by the third one, he'd figured it out.

He was a little winded when he landed at the end, and his arm muscles were feeling the strain of the unusual movements. But he didn't hesitate, moving on to the Loco Ladder.

This obstacle had been on the show, too. It was like a giant pegboard. He was supposed to grab the two metal rods sticking out of the lowest holes on the board, then move them one at a time into higher holes to climb the wall, with his entire body weight dangling from his hands. A ninja had to be both strong and precise to conquer this obstacle.

"You can do it, Noah!" Mackenzie yelled.

Noah hoped she was right. He jumped up and grabbed the rods, then hung there for a moment, measuring the space to the next hole with his eyes. Somehow it looked farther than it had from below. But all he could do was try.

He yanked the right-hand peg out of its hole, aiming at the higher one. But it glanced off the edge instead of going in.

"Aargh!" he cried as he felt his other hand slip. He tried to hang on, but it was no use.

"Good try, Noah!" Mackenzie called as Noah hit the

mat, tucking and rolling automatically. "That's a hard obstacle."

"It is," Coach Tara agreed, hurrying forward. "You okay? Looks like you know how to take a fall, anyway."

Noah forced a smile. "Yeah. That's one of the first things we learn in dance."

Tara chuckled. "Well, good. That's one thing we won't have to worry about, then." She grinned at him. "Welcome to the team, Noah!"

Nine

JJ STEPPED FORWARD with Mackenzie and Kevin to trade fist bumps with Noah. "Nice going," he said. "I'm JJ."

"I know." The new kid shot him a brief smile. "You were great on the show."

"Thanks." JJ grinned. "Looks like you'll be giving me some competition!"

Mackenzie laughed. But Izzy and Kevin just traded a look.

Ty rolled his eyes. "Can we get back to work now?" he grumbled.

JJ wasn't sure why Ty was acting so cranky. It would be fun having someone new on the team. Besides, Noah seemed nice. JJ didn't know much about dancing, but the kid seemed to have some skills. He'd looked almost as good as JJ himself scrambling up the climbing wall, and even better than Izzy on the balance log.

But there was no time to worry about it. Tara put them back to work right away, including Noah, and for the rest of the session JJ didn't have the energy to think about anything except what he was doing.

"How was ninja practice today?" JJ's mom asked when he came into the kitchen a few hours later. Jasmine was there, too, sitting at the table reading a book.

"Great." JJ hurried straight to the fridge for a drink. "We got a new team member."

"Really?" His sister looked up from her book, brushing a strand of blond hair out of her face. "What do you mean?"

JJ took a gulp of his sports drink before answering.

"Close the door, JJ," his mother scolded.

"Sorry." JJ kicked the refrigerator door shut, then collapsed into the seat across from Jasmine. "It's a kid who heard about the wildcard thing and decided he wants to try out. So he's on our team now."

"Anyone we know?" his mother asked.

"I don't think so." JJ shrugged. "His name's Noah — he goes to Izzy's school. He's, like, some awesome dancer or something. At least that's what Mack says."

Jasmine sat up straighter. "Wait — are you talking about

Noah Dhawan?" she said. "Tall, skinny Indian kid, right? I know him! He was in that production of *Mary Poppins* I was in last year."

"Was he?" Their mother tilted her head to one side, the way she always did when she was trying to remember something. "Did he play your brother?"

"No. He didn't have a speaking role or anything." Jasmine shook her head. "He was just in the dance corps. But his mom was the director."

"Really?" JJ thought back to the play. His parents had insisted that the whole family go every night it was on so that they could support Jasmine. He remembered it pretty well. "I thought that red-haired lady who came out at the end was the director. That's Noah's mom? Is he adopted or something?"

"No. His dad's Indian," Jasmine explained. "Stella moved to India to marry him, actually." She frowned. "Which is too bad, since it's probably the reason she's not a movie star right now."

JJ took another sip of his drink. "What do you mean?"

"Stella's acting career was just taking off when they met," Jasmine said. "She was starting to get national commercials and even had a walk-on part in some big TV sitcom." She shrugged. "But then she moved to India for like ten years, and by the time they moved back here, she couldn't get much work anymore."

"How romantic," JJ's mother said. "She gave up her career for love."

"I guess." Jasmine didn't sound impressed. "Anyway, Noah's a great dancer. I wonder why he's bothering with this ninja stuff, though — he's pretty busy."

"Maybe because it's fun?" JJ said.

Before his sister or mother could answer, the door opened and JJ's dad hurried in. "Ah, there you are." He pointed at JJ. "You know Mr. Wolfe, right?"

"Sure — from the coffee shop?" JJ knew that his father and uncle had been working on Mr. Wolfe's renovations for the past month. The two of them were contractors — no job too big or too small.

"Uh-huh. We're wrapping up the job tomorrow, and the ribbon cutting's the day after." Mr. Johnson grinned at JJ. "And he asked if the town's newest ninja superstar would do the honors."

"Huh?" For a second, JJ didn't understand. "Wait — you mean he wants me to cut the ribbon? You're joking, right?"

"No joke, son." His father stepped over and ruffled JJ's short blond hair. "You're a local celebrity now, you know. Why get the boring old mayor to do a ribbon cutting when you could get a real-life ninja?"

"Wow." Jasmine looked almost as surprised as JJ felt. "I've never been asked to do anything like that."

She sounded a little envious, which made JJ feel kind

of weird. He was pretty sure his smart, multitalented older sister had never been envious of him in their whole lives. But he decided not to worry about it. His sister was always winning all different kinds of awards and honors. Maybe it was time for him to get to do something special.

His father was still watching him, smiling. “So what do you say, son?”

JJ grinned. “I say get me some scissors! Hey — maybe I can even convince the rest of the team to come, too!”

Ten

PUSH THROUGH IT!" Coach Tara yelled. "Go — you can do it!"

Izzy gritted her teeth and tightened her grip. Tara was making them climb the big, ceiling-height cargo net without using their feet. Izzy's arms were burning, her hands raw from the rope. But finally she made it to the top.

"Good job," Tara said. "Noah, you're up."

Izzy climbed down — using her feet as much as possible this time — and collapsed on the floor beside Kevin.

"He's good, isn't he?" Kevin said as he watched Noah tackle the cargo rope.

"He's fit, that's for sure," Izzy said.

She still wasn't sure what to think about Noah. Ty wasn't

happy about the newcomer — he was making no secret of that. But the others seemed to be okay with him. And so far he was keeping up with the rest of the team, even though Tara was working them pretty hard. He'd made it up the Crazy Cliff on his second day and was starting to get the hang of the Loco Ladder.

He's good, I guess, Izzy thought. *I just hope he doesn't mess up the team spirit thing we have going on.* She sneaked a look at Ty, who was scowling as he watched Noah scale the net.

After Noah finished, it was JJ's turn and then Mackenzie's. Finally Tara seemed satisfied. "Water break, everyone," she said. "We'll pick up in ten."

Izzy climbed to her feet and wandered over to her gym duffel. She grabbed her phone along with her water bottle, checking her texts.

Her eyes widened when she saw that there was one from Jess. A couple of days had passed since they'd run into each other, and Izzy had just about decided that Jess was finished with her. But maybe not. She clicked the text open and scanned it.

> Hey, you've heard about the big LD party down at the quarry, right? Wanna go?

Izzy turned away to hide her grin. She didn't want the others to see how psyched she was or to start asking questions. She was pretty sure that none of them would get an invite to this particular party. Not until they were in high school, anyway. Besides, she'd have to sneak out to go, and she didn't want too many people knowing about that, just in case.

The quarry party was legendary. It happened every year to celebrate the end of summer on the Friday of Labor Day weekend.

Labor Day weekend. Suddenly Izzy's heart sank.

"Oh, no," she mumbled.

Mackenzie glanced up from her water. "What? Did you say something, Iz?" she asked.

"No, nothing." Izzy quickly clicked off her phone and shoved it back in her bag.

The Friday of Labor Day weekend — that was the night before they were all leaving for the finals. Their flight to the West Coast left at some ridiculously early hour on Saturday morning. How would she manage that if she was out all night at the quarry party?

Mackenzie was still watching her. "Are you all right?" she asked.

"I'm fine, okay?" Izzy snapped.

The younger girl looked slightly wounded, but Izzy hardly noticed. Her head was spinning as she tried to figure out how she was going to make this work. Because if she didn't make it to that party, Jess would probably never invite her to anything cool ever again.

Eleven

"THIS IS SO COOL!" Mackenzie exclaimed as she climbed out of the Fit Kidz van with her teammates and Tara. "It's like we're real celebrities!"

She smiled and waved to the crowd gathered in front of Wolfe's Coffee Cup. At first, when JJ told them about the ribbon cutting, everyone thought it was a joke. Everyone except Tara, that is. She told them it was pretty normal for someone who'd appeared on TV to get asked to do stuff like that. Once, she had even been asked to help welcome a new giraffe to the local zoo!

"I'm not sure *cool* is the right word," Ty grumbled, swiping the sweat off his brow with the back of his arm. "It's like a heat wave out here."

All five of them were wearing the same outfits they'd worn on the show. As soon as they appeared, a couple of photographers stepped forward to take pictures of them. A crowd had gathered to watch the ceremony, and several people cheered when they spotted the kids.

"Ninja champions!" a young man yelled, pumping his fist.

"Yeah!" Ty yelled back.

JJ's dad bustled over. "Ready to get started, kids?" he asked.

"Sure!" Mackenzie said. She liked JJ's dad. He'd helped to adjust the equipment at the gym for the new ninja team, and she had enjoyed joking around with him while he was there.

JJ's dad led the ninjas over to the coffee shop's entrance. A huge red ribbon was hanging across the front of the building, and Mackenzie snapped a few photos with her phone. She wanted to put this on her blog later.

"Over here, Mayor!" Mr. Wolfe called, waving to a slender woman in a red pantsuit.

"Is that really the mayor?" Kevin asked.

"Sure." Mackenzie waved to Mayor Fuentes. "My birth mom went to high school with her. She's really nice."

"Hello, young ninjas!" The mayor was all smiles as she joined them beside the ribbon. "I saw your show. Some of those stunts made me tired just watching them!"

All the adults standing nearby chuckled.

"It's really fun," Mackenzie told the mayor. "You should come to the gym and try it sometime."

"Oh, not me!" The mayor winked. "I get winded just walking from my office to the car!"

"I used to say I was allergic to exercise," Mackenzie told her, "but being a ninja isn't like most exercise. It's a blast!"

Mr. Wolfe cleared his throat. "Shall we begin?" he asked, mopping his brow with a handkerchief. He snapped his fingers, and a young man hurried over, holding a giant pair of scissors. He handed them to the mayor, but she turned to smile at the kids.

"Who wants to do the honors?" she asked.

Mr. Wolfe suggested that the ninjas and the mayor all cut the ribbon together. Mackenzie pressed forward with her teammates, reaching out to put a hand on the handle of the giant scissors.

"One . . . two . . . three . . ." the mayor counted.

SNAP! The ribbon broke as soon as the scissors touched it. The crowd cheered, and Mr. Wolfe beamed as the photographers took more pictures.

After that, a bunch of people came forward to talk to the ninja team and their coach. Some of them had questions about certain obstacles or what it was like to be on TV. Others wanted to ask for the kids' autographs or to take selfies with them.

Mackenzie felt like a real celebrity now. She signed her name so many times that her hand got sore. She also posed for lots of pictures with her fans. It was fun at first, but it was an awfully hot day. After half an hour or so, Mackenzie was starting to feel sweaty and tired. Still, she tried not to let her fans see that.

"So girls can be ninjas too, huh?" a middle-aged woman asked, glancing from Mackenzie to Izzy to Tara.

"Um, sure," Mackenzie said.

"No, we're all actually boys in disguise," Izzy snapped at the same time.

The woman looked startled. Tara cleared her throat. "She's joking," she told the woman with a quick smile. Then she put one hand on Izzy's back and the other on Mackenzie's and steered them away from the woman. "Maybe it's time to wrap this up," she called to JJ's dad.

"Thanks for coming, everyone," he called out. "Let's have a hand for our young ninja champions!"

"And Wolfe's Coffee Cup!" Mr. Wolfe added as the crowd cheered.

Noah was doing chin-ups when Mackenzie and the others walked into the ninja room a few minutes later. Ty's mother was there, spotting him.

"Wow, he's hardcore," JJ commented.

Mackenzie wasn't surprised that their newest teammate was taking this seriously. Daddy Jim had told her once that Noah took four or five dance classes every week and practiced for hours every day.

"Whatever." Ty sounded cranky. "I need to hydrate."

As Ty and the others went to grab sports drinks from the cooler by the door, Mackenzie wandered toward Noah. "Hi," she said. "I guess you got a head start today."

"Uh-huh," he said, dropping to the floor and flexing his hands. "How was the ribbon cutting?"

"Fun. You should have come."

"It's okay." Noah glanced around the room. "I want to make sure I'm ready to kill at those tryouts. And the finals after that."

"Wow, you sound confident!" Mackenzie exclaimed, a little surprised. "I mean, you always seem kind of, you know, quiet and shy. But you don't even seem nervous about this!"

"Oh, I'm plenty nervous," Noah responded with a smile. "But that's normal, right? Anyway, my favorite dance teacher always tells me to visualize doing it right. So that's what I'm doing."

"Cool." Mackenzie made a mental note to remember that tip. "If it helps, I can totally visualize you killing it on that tryout course—just like you always kill it onstage."

Twelve

"READY FOR THIS?" Coach Tara asked.

Noah nodded and looked around the crowded North Creek gym. It was the day of the wildcard tryouts, and he felt pretty confident. He'd been working hard at Fit Kidz every day, focusing on conquering every obstacle he might face on course. It was similar to learning a new dance routine—practicing the different steps and movements one at a time and then putting them together.

"Thanks for coming with me to tryouts," he told Tara.

"Of course." She smiled. "I wouldn't miss it."

Noah smiled back. He liked Tara—she reminded him a little bit of his favorite dance teacher. They were both tough and focused but also peppy and positive.

"It's pretty crowded, huh?" He glanced around again. "Was it this bad at the first tryouts?"

"Almost." Tara dodged to avoid being run into by an anxious-looking kid dressed in a karate outfit. "I'm not surprised it's packed today, since the show has been such a big hit."

Noah nodded. He'd watched the second episode of *JNC* a few nights earlier, and there had been an announcement at the end about the wildcard show. He figured Tara was right—it had brought lots more wannabe ninjas out of the woodwork, just the way an open audition for a show always did.

He scanned the room, wondering who his competition would be. Some of the kids standing in line to sign up didn't look very athletic. Some even looked older or younger than the ages allowed. There was a boy made up like a clown with the words BOZO NINJA emblazoned on his T-shirt, and a girl wearing a mermaid's tail. Plenty of anxious or excited or bored parents and friends were hanging around while local reporters recorded the whole chaotic scene.

It took a few minutes to sign in and get his number. Then Noah and Tara passed through an arched doorway into the main part of the gym. The course was set up at one end, with a warm-up area at the other.

"Why don't you start your warm-up while I check out the course," Tara suggested. "We can go over it together in a few."

"Sounds good." As Tara hurried off, Noah found a free mat and did a few stretches, doing his best to ignore the chaos surrounding him. After all, it was no worse than being backstage on opening night.

"Noah! Oh my gosh, is that you?"

Noah glanced up at the sound of his name. A pretty girl with a reddish-blond ponytail was rushing toward him. For a second he didn't recognize her. Then she came closer, and he realized it was Chloe O'Neal. She was a dancer and an actress who had played one of the younger daughters in the recent production of *Fiddler on the Roof*. She was fairly new in town, so Noah didn't know her that well. But his mother already adored her, saying that Chloe reminded her of herself when she was thirteen.

"Hi," Noah said. "What are you doing here?"

"What do you think? Auditioning, just like you!" Chloe let out a tinkly laugh and tossed her ponytail back over her shoulder. "This is crazy, right?"

"I guess." Noah glanced at the girl's outfit, which consisted of white capri pants and a fluttery pale-blue blouse. "If you're trying out, you should probably change clothes."

"What?" Chloe looked down at herself. "Oh, no. This should be fine. This color looks really good on me on camera. This same outfit helped me land an ad for a local pizza place!" She giggled. "Besides, I don't do sweatpants."

Noah didn't say anything, returning to his stretching. He wasn't sure that Chloe realized what kind of tryout this was. Did she even know anything about being a ninja, or had she just heard this was a chance to be on TV?

"So a little birdie told me you're trying out for *Beauty and the Beast* next month," Chloe singsonged. "Is it true you're going for Chip?"

"What?" Noah blurted out. "Where did you hear that?" Chip was a major role, with solo lines in a couple of songs. Besides, the part didn't involve any real dancing at all! Why in the world would he want to try out for it?

Chloe smirked and pantomimed zipping her lips. But that was okay. Noah was pretty sure he knew exactly who was telling people that he was trying out for a major role in the next play . . .

Just then Tara hurried over. "Ready to walk the course?" she asked Noah, not seeming to notice Chloe standing there.

"I'm ready." Noah jumped to his feet. "Let's go."

Thirteen

"THERE HE IS!" Mackenzie cried, jumping up and down for a better view over the heads of the spectators crowded around the tryout course. "Noah! Whoooo!"

Noah had just stepped onto the start mat. Tara was talking to him. But at Mackenzie's shout, they both looked over, their faces startled.

Mackenzie grinned and waved, thrilled that she'd surprised them. She'd convinced Papa Kurt to drive her over to support Noah in his tryouts. It was fun to be back in the North Creek gym — it was even noisier and hotter and more crowded than she remembered from her own tryouts, but she loved it! This course was a little different from the other one, just as the producers had promised. Mackenzie wished she could try some of the new obstacles, especially a cool balance obstacle called Wall to Wall. Instead, she'd settled for taking lots of pictures to show her teammates later.

"This is fun, right?" she said, elbowing her father, who was beside her in the crowd of onlookers. "I wish some of the others had decided to come."

For a second, her sunny mood faded a little. She'd invited the rest of the ninja team to join in her surprise. But all four of them had said no.

Papa Kurt shot her an understanding look. "Don't worry about it, Mack," he said. "I'm sure it means a lot to Noah that you're here."

"Yeah." Mackenzie bit her lip, glancing at Noah. He was still on the mat, watching the ninja before him, a lanky boy with a fauxhawk who was a couple of obstacles into the course. "And I guess maybe JJ would have come if he wasn't busy meeting that client of his dad's who saw him at the ribbon cutting."

"JJ seems like a nice kid," Papa Kurt said.

"And Kevin had to go to his brother's piano recital," Mackenzie went on. She frowned. "But the other two didn't have good excuses. When I told Izzy I wanted to support Noah, she just said she'd start supporting him if and when he actually makes the wildcard show."

Papa Kurt rubbed his chin. "Hmm."

"Still, I guess at least she'll give him a chance then,"

Mackenzie said. "Ty doesn't seem to want Noah on the team at all! When I asked if he wanted to come along today, he said no way!"

"Ty's used to winning," Papa Kurt said. "Your uncle Leo was the same way as a kid. But he got over it, and I bet Ty will, too."

"You think so?" Mackenzie watched the fauxhawk ninja struggling to make it through the fourth obstacle, a rope-climbing one. "Maybe. I just don't get him sometimes."

Papa Kurt patted her shoulder. "You guys are all pretty different, aren't you? But maybe that's why you make such a good team."

Mackenzie thought about that. Maybe her father was right. Ty was supercompetitive — that was his thing. Just like her thing was getting everyone revved up and excited, and Kevin's was working hard, and JJ's was being laid-back and positive, and Izzy's was staying cool, calm, and collected. If they were all the same, maybe their team wouldn't work so well . . .

She forgot about that when the fauxhawk kid finally lost his grip on the ropes and fell to the mats below. The crowd groaned with sympathy. As the kid left the course, a woman with a clipboard gestured to Noah, and Tara stepped back off the start mat.

"Here he goes," Mackenzie said, crossing her fingers as Noah stepped forward.

Fourteen

NOAH SHOT ONE last glance toward Mackenzie on the sidelines, still surprised that she was there. She was a nice person — he should have known she'd want to support him.

Unlike the rest of my so-called team, he thought.

But he shook his head quickly, doing his best to banish negative thoughts. He needed to focus, to visualize a positive result. Besides, what was the big deal? He was used to cutthroat competition from the theater world, where a dozen other dancers were always waiting for you to mess up, twist your ankle, or get sick so they could grab your role.

"Whenever you're ready, ninja," the woman with the clipboard said.

Noah nodded. He was ready.

The first obstacle was a set of balance steps. Noah skipped through them easily, then moved on to the bar swings that came next. It reminded him of the trapeze work he'd done in a dance class a few years before, and when he dismounted, he was smiling. That had been fun!

The third obstacle was a tricky balance bridge that had taken out a lot of people so far. The beam was narrow and made several turns and changes in height. But it was a piece of cake for Noah, and soon he found himself facing the ropes obstacle that had taken out the previous ninja.

"Gooooo, Noah!" Mackenzie cried, her voice cutting through the noise of the crowd.

Noah barely heard her as he studied the task ahead of him. The first part of the obstacle involved shimmying up a thick rope. Then you had to grab the first of a series of shorter ropes, swinging across them all to a rope ladder. There were no knots on the shorter ropes, which made them hard to grip.

"Slow and easy, Noah!" Tara shouted from her spot on the sidelines.

He glanced at the coach and nodded. Then he leaped up and grabbed the long rope, ignoring the way the rough fibers rubbed his hands and legs.

Getting to the top wasn't too hard. But once he was up there, the first of the short ropes looked impossibly far away. How was he supposed to reach it?

He closed his eyes for a second, picturing the ropes at Fit Kidz. For some reason, he found himself remembering a day last week when Ty had been messing around up there, acting like Tarzan and swinging around one-handed.

Noah's eyes flew open as he realized what he needed to do. He had to use his body weight to get the long rope swinging, just as Ty had done that day. He did it, and was able to reach the short rope on the first swing. His momentum carried him onto the next rope, and the next.

After that, the rest of the course seemed to fly by. He'd worked hard to master the Loco Ladder, and after that came a balance exercise that involved jumping from the top of one narrow wall to another. Finally came the Crazy Cliff—and as Noah flew up the steep wall, he was already grinning. Mission accomplished!

"Good news, Noah." Tara rushed up to the Fit Kidz van, where Noah and Mrs. Santiago were waiting. Mackenzie was there, too—she'd stayed for the whole tryouts.

"Did he make it through to the wildcard show?" Mackenzie asked.

"Not only that." Tara grinned. "He had the fastest time of the day!"

"Awesome!" Mackenzie lifted her hand.

Noah high-fived her. "Thanks," he said. "Wow—the fastest? Really?"

Mackenzie laughed. "You must have visualized like crazy! Now all you have to do is visualize winning the finals, too!"

"Congrats, Noah," Tara said, raising an eyebrow at Mackenzie. "Don't let this make you overconfident, though. It will take more than positive visualization to make sure you're ready for the wildcard show, never mind the finals. It'll take a lot of hard work, too."

Noah nodded, but he wasn't really focused on the coach's words. He was used to working hard. Right now he was just thinking about how excited his mother was going to be to see him on TV.

Fifteen

"READY TO GET STARTED?" Tara asked, striding into the ninja room on Tuesday morning. "We have a lot to do today."

Ty had been doing pushups to warm up. Now he jumped to his feet, feeling pumped. "Let's do this!" he cried.

"Wait." Mackenzie looked up from her cell phone. "Noah's not here yet."

Tara nodded. "He texted to say he'll be a little late," she said. "He has his weekly voice lesson today."

"Voice lesson?" Ty made a face. "Are you serious?"

"Yes." Tara raised her eyebrows at him. "Do you have a problem with that?"

"Nope." But Ty didn't mean it. He definitely had a problem with just about everything Noah did.

I mean, I gave up an entire season of travel soccer to be a ninja, he thought with a grimace. *And this kid won't even skip one lousy voice lesson a few days before the wildcard filming?*

But he didn't dare say any of that in front of Tara and the others. Ever since the tryouts on Saturday, Mackenzie hadn't been able to stop talking about how Noah had aced the course. That seemed to make the others think he was part of the team now. But Ty still wasn't ready to accept that. He didn't think it was fair that Noah had a chance to make the finals and he didn't.

Ty realized that Tara was talking again, and he tuned back in.

". . . and Ty's dad will drive the van up to the university again, just like last time," she was saying. "We'll all meet here at the gym at six thirty."

"Wait — what?" Ty said. "Um, what did you say?"

Kevin glanced at him. "She's talking about Saturday. You know, the filming?"

"We're all going?" Ty blurted out.

"Sure." JJ shrugged. "I mean, aren't we?"

Suddenly everyone seemed to be looking at Ty. For a second he wasn't sure what to say. Why did they all assume he was coming? Why should he wake up early on a Saturday and ride halfway across the state in a stuffy van just to cheer Noah on? It wasn't as if he actually wanted the kid to do well . . .

But he couldn't say that in front of the others. Especially Tara.

"Um, okay," he muttered instead. "So what time did you say to meet here?"

"Six thirty," Kevin said, and Ty nodded.

Whatever. Come to think of it, maybe it would be kind of fun to see Noah choke.

"Whoa, he's good!" JJ exclaimed.

Ty nodded, but he didn't take his eyes off the TV. It was Thursday night, and the whole ninja team was gathered at the Fit Kidz gym to watch the third episode of *Junior Ninja Champion*. A tall, broad-shouldered black kid named Benjamin Turay was on course. His nickname was Benny the Beast, and Ty could see why. Benny had powered through the first six obstacles as if they were nothing.

"Yeah, he's going to be one to watch in the finals," Kevin said.

"He hasn't made it yet," Ty said. "Anyway, I bet I could beat him. You know — if I get called in."

"Maybe," Izzy said. "He's pretty good."

Onscreen, Benny stepped up to the seventh obstacle, a set of balance blocks called Tiptoe Tulips.

"Beast! Beast! Beast!" Mackenzie chanted, pumping her fist as Benny leaped onto the first block.

Noah leaned forward, watching carefully. "This guy's good, but he's kind of top-heavy," he said. "Lots of muscles. See? He doesn't look totally solid on this one. Bet all the balance obstacles are tough for him."

Ty shot him an irritated look. He'd almost forgotten that the newbie was there — Noah hadn't come to last week's viewing, but he'd already been sitting with the others tonight when Ty had come in from sweeping up the hallway. He guessed Mackenzie must have invited him.

"You really think you can beat that guy?" Ty challenged Noah.

Noah shrugged. "Sure, why not?" he replied quietly. "Nobody's perfect."

Izzy laughed. "True. So maybe you'd better make the finals first, okay?"

Noah didn't say anything, and Ty smirked. Then he returned his attention to Benny, who had just made it up the Crazy Cliff to wild cheers from the crowd. It was always good to keep an eye on the competition.

Sixteen

"GETTING NERVOUS?" KEVIN ASKED.

He glanced over at Noah, who was sitting between him and JJ in the middle seat of the van. It was Saturday, and they were halfway to the state university, where one of the wildcard tapings would take place.

Noah shrugged, staring out the window at the highway scenery sliding past. "Sure, a little," he said. "But I'm used to it from auditions and stuff."

"Oh, right." JJ nodded. Then he laughed. "I wasn't nervous at all last time. But that's because I thought I was just an alternate!"

"Really?" Noah said.

Kevin smiled, thinking back to that day. "I was definitely nervous," he said. "But excited, too. We all were."

He glanced around the van. Ty's mom was driving, and his dad was in the passenger seat. Izzy, Mackenzie, and Tara were sitting in the first seat behind that. Then came Kevin and the other two, and finally Ty, who was lounging on the back seat, listening to headphones.

"Anyway, if you do get nervous, just remember that the whole team will be out there cheering you on," Kevin told Noah.

"Really?" Noah glanced over, his dark eyes surprised. "Um, I wasn't sure everyone was that psyched to have me around."

"Sure we are," JJ said quickly.

"Yeah," Kevin said. He had a feeling he knew what Noah was thinking—not everybody had been that welcoming. He glanced over his shoulder briefly, though Ty didn't notice. "Listen, don't let anyone make you think you're not part of the team, okay?"

"Right," JJ said. "We've really helped each other through some stuff. I was pretty freaked out when I got called in as an alternate at the last minute."

"Yeah, and I wasn't sure I'd be able to compete at all," Kevin added, thinking back to what had happened. "My mom didn't exactly know about the whole ninja thing at first. I wasn't sure she'd let me go to the semifinals taping."

Noah looked curious. "Really? Why wouldn't she?"

Kevin thought about how to explain his mother to someone who'd never met her. "You know I had cancer when I was younger, right?" When Noah nodded, Kevin went on. "She sometimes forgets that I beat it — that I'm fine now. That I can do anything other kids do."

JJ reached across Noah to clap Kevin on the shoulder. "So Izzy convinced her to come see Kev do his thing. She was so impressed that she said he could do it."

"Yeah. I was mad at first, because Izzy went behind my back to tell her. But she was right. It was the best way to show my mom what I'm capable of and how much I really wanted to be a ninja."

JJ nodded. "I guess your parents couldn't make it today, huh?" he asked Noah. "Or are they driving up separately?"

"They're not coming," Noah said. "But listen — do you guys have any tips for the Loco Ladder? That's still the toughest thing for me."

"Sure!" JJ said eagerly. "That one took me a while to get, too. Here's what I did . . ."

As JJ chattered away, Kevin shot Noah a sidelong glance. Was it his imagination, or had Noah been pretty quick to change the subject away from his parents?

I guess it's none of my business, Kevin told himself. *But maybe I'm not the only one with a complicated family . . .*

• • •

A few hours later, Kevin cheered loudly as a ninja attacked the tire swing obstacle. It was fun watching the competition without the pressure of competing himself. Sort of like watching the other semifinals shows on TV — except better! The producers had changed up the course for the wildcard show, since they didn't want the competitors to be able to practice ahead of time. A few obstacles were the same as the ones Kevin and his other teammates had gone up against, while others were brand-new.

"Awww," Kevin groaned along with the rest of the onlookers when the ninja fell on the second tire.

"That tire thing looks even trickier than ours was," Izzy commented. "I hope Noah's paying attention, or his career as a ninja will be over fast."

Kevin nodded. Noah had gone off with Tara to get warmed up for his round, which was coming up soon. Ty had disappeared, too, though Kevin didn't know where.

A petite girl stepped onto the mat. When her package played, Kevin and the others learned that her name was Chen Chang — also known as the Mighty Mini because of her tiny size.

"Wow, she's even smaller than Tara," Mackenzie commented.

"Yeah. Let's see if she's as good," JJ said with a grin.

The answer seemed to be yes. From the moment she raced across the balance poles that started the course, Chen barely slowed down to take a breath.

"Wow!" JJ shouted when the Mighty Mini leaped to her feet at the top of the Crazy Cliff. "She absolutely destroyed that course!"

Mackenzie elbowed JJ with a grin. "Looks like she'll be one of the ninjas to beat in the finals."

"For sure!" JJ agreed.

"I wonder why she didn't try out the first time around," Kevin added.

"Maybe she didn't hear about it in time," JJ said. "We might not have either if Mack hadn't told us."

Meanwhile, Izzy was looking toward the start mat. "Check it out — Noah's up next."

Seventeen

NOAH COULDN'T BELIEVE he had to follow Chen the Mighty Mini. The whole place had erupted in wild shouts and applause halfway through her course, and it hadn't quieted down much by the time his own package started to play.

He glanced up at the screen. He'd managed to convince his dad not to tell his mother about the filming of his package. They'd arranged for it to happen while she was out of town for the day. Would she be mad when she found out? And what about when she found out about today's taping? Would she be upset that he hadn't told her about that, either? Or would she accept that he'd wanted it to be a surprise.

"Ready?" Tara asked, interrupting his thoughts.

Noah nodded, then jumped up and down a few times, shaking out his arms and legs. "Begin whenever you're ready, ninja," said the woman standing by the start.

Noah took a step forward, eyeing the first obstacle, known as the Leaning Poles of Pizza. It consisted of six wooden poles of varying heights, most of the them slanted to some degree. They stuck up from a large, colorful pizza painted on the floor, as if the poles were warped stacks of pepperoni.

The cheers and whistles from the crowd hadn't died down, but Noah knew they weren't for him—they were for Chen, who was standing with her coach near the base of the Crazy Cliff. He couldn't help feeling a little rattled by all the commotion, but he did his best to ignore it as he took a deep breath and jumped up onto the first pole, which was only slightly slanted.

Tara had advised him to try to get through as quickly as possible, so Noah pushed off the first pole immediately, aiming for the second, taller pole. The tops were small, no larger than the top of an average fencepost, and his foot hit it slightly askew. Noah wobbled, swinging his arms to keep his balance, and shoved himself forward toward the third pole, which was shorter and very slanted.

The rest of the poles went okay, though Noah felt a little unbalanced the whole way through. When he finally landed safely on the mat at the end, he stood there for a second, trying to regain his composure. Out of the corner of his eye he saw Chen walking past him toward the locker rooms, waving to cheering fans.

Focus, Noah told himself. *Get your head back in the game or this was all for nothing.*

The second obstacle was called Hanging Out. It was a large, squared-off log, its edges set on a pair of sloped metal tracks. Ninjas were supposed to hang on to it upside down as it slid down the tracks. Several competitors had lost their grip halfway down, and others had been shaken loose when it hit the end of the tracks, falling into the safety net instead of throwing themselves forward onto the landing mat.

Noah wrapped his arms and legs around the obstacle and pushed off. His muscles were strong from years of dance, and he had little trouble hanging on and reaching the mat. After that came an obstacle that involved grabbing balls that were hanging from chains and then swinging across.

Next came the Loco Ladder. Noah wiped his hands on his shorts, staring up at it. He flashed back to that first day at Fit Kidz, when he'd messed it up. There was probably no obstacle he'd practiced more, and he was sure he could conquer it this time.

Finals, here we come, he thought as he leaped up to grab the pegs.

But he soon realized that this was going to be harder than it looked. The holes on this Loco Ladder were farther apart than the ones at the gym. The first time he aimed for a new hole, he came up a couple of inches short and almost lost his grip.

Mackenzie's voice floated to him over the crowd noise. "Take it easy, Noah!"

Noah shoved the peg back into the first hole and closed his eyes, catching his breath and visualizing what he needed to do. Then he opened his eyes and tried again. This time he made it—but just barely. He was going to have to take his time; there was no room for error.

Finally, what felt like a lifetime later, he made it to the top. The crowd cheered, but Noah barely heard it. At least the next obstacle should be easier. It was a set of balance steps called Stepping Out, and he recognized it from seeing it on TV. Most of his teammates hadn't had much trouble with it, and neither did he. He made it through the tire swing obstacle, too, along with another balance obstacle called the Swirly Steps, which were spinning disks on poles.

After that, all he had to do was make it up the Crazy Cliff. "Climb that Cliff! Climb that Cliff!" the crowd chanted.

Noah wanted to get it over with. But he was a little winded from the rest of the course, and he forced himself to stop and catch his breath.

Then he noticed a commotion in the crowd. He glanced over and saw Chen surrounded by fans and reporters. Thinking about how fast she'd made it through the course reminded him that he'd lost a lot of time on the Loco Ladder. He hadn't been particularly quick through the tire swings, either. Only ten ninjas would make the finals from all six wildcard locations. How many others had already completed the course, and how fast had they done it? He had no idea . . .

Suddenly panicked at the thought of missing his goal, he gulped in one last deep breath and ran at the Crazy Cliff.

At the first step up the steep wall, he could feel that he didn't have quite as much momentum as he'd hoped. *No!* He couldn't miss this chance . . .

Calling on every ounce of strength and body control he had, he pushed himself up, up, up . . . His hands scrabbled for the lip of the cliff. His right hand came up just short, but he managed to get three fingers of his left hand over . . .

Seconds later Noah collapsed on top of the Crazy Cliff, gulping for breath and hardly daring to believe he'd made it. But would it be enough?

Eighteen

IZZY WAS WATCHING a tall boy struggle to make it up the Loco Ladder when her phone vibrated in her pocket. She pulled it out and saw that it was a text from Jess giving a few more details about the Labor Day party.

She scanned it, then clicked off her phone, not wanting to think about the party right then. She still hadn't decided what to do.

"Ohhh!" the crowd sighed.

Glancing up, Izzy saw that the tall ninja had just fallen. "That's the last person," she said. Kevin and Noah nodded. The two of them had wandered over to join her a few minutes earlier.

"Only four ninjas finished the course in our location,"

Kevin said. "And that one girl was really slow the whole way through. That means you've got a great shot at the finals, Noah."

"Yeah," Izzy added. "It depends on how many made it through in the other five wildcard locations, I guess. Anyway, we'll find out soon."

Noah nodded, but didn't say anything. Izzy could see that his hands were shaking.

"Nervous, huh?" she said. "I don't blame you. But you did what you could, right?"

At first Izzy hadn't been sure that the Fit Kidz team really needed another member, especially since Noah's arrival had turned Ty into a grumpy grouch. But that was Ty's problem, right? Anyway, Noah had won Izzy over. He was a hard worker, and he really seemed to want this. So what if it meant more competition if he actually made the finals? Izzy had never been supercompetitive the way Ty was. Being a ninja was about beating the obstacles and testing your limits, not about winning. Then again, she knew not everyone saw it that way.

Noah shrugged. "I just wish I had made better time."

At that moment Mellie Monroe appeared on the big screen where the competitors' packages played. She had been hosting live at the West Coast semis, so this was the first time Izzy and the others had seen her. "May I have your attention please," Mellie said. "I have the list of ninjas from all six wildcard locations who are invited to compete in the finals in Los Angeles. Those ninjas are: Chen Chang . . ."

She had to pause, since the place went wild at the mention of the Mighty Mini's name. When it quieted down, Mellie continued, listing eight other names. Izzy held her breath.

". . . and finally, Noah Dhawan," the host finished. "Congratulations to all our ninjas! We'll see you in California!"

Ten wildcard ninjas had made it. That meant Ty was out of luck. Izzy glanced around to see how he was taking it, but he was nowhere in sight.

"Congratulations!" Kevin said to Noah, grinning. "See? Told you you had a shot."

"Yeah," Izzy said, smiling at Noah. "Don't look so shocked. Or are you scared 'cause now you have to compete against me?"

Noah laughed, but then he shook his head. "Wow. I didn't think I'd make it after I messed up at the Loco Ladder. I've never been this nervous waiting for a result."

"You mean like at dance auditions or whatever?" Izzy tried to remember what Mackenzie had said about Noah. "No surprise there. I mean, you've been doing that forever, right? So you must be really good. And you just became a ninja a few weeks ago."

"Yeah, I've been dancing forever." Noah shrugged.

"Singing and acting, too, but that doesn't make me any good at those things."

"What do you mean?" Kevin asked. "Mack says you're always in the local musicals and stuff."

"I am — as a dancer." Noah grimaced. "Even though my mom wishes I could be more like her."

Izzy was curious now. Noah hardly ever talked about himself or his family. "What do you mean, more like her?" she asked.

"She's supertalented at everything — singing, dancing, acting," Noah said with a sigh. "She's had me taking lessons for all that stuff for as long as I can remember — trying to turn me into a star. That's a big part of why we moved back here from India when I was little. She thought both of us would have more opportunities to work in show business here. She convinced my dad to look for a job at a lab over here, and voilà! Here we are."

"Oh." Izzy could tell that Noah wasn't happy about what he was saying. "So I guess you'd rather live in India, huh?" she asked.

Noah shook his head. "That's not it," he said. "I just wish — "

"Noah! There you are!" JJ shouted, rushing over to them. Mackenzie, Ty, and Tara were right on his heels. Ty was glowering, which didn't surprise Izzy one bit — she knew he had to be bummed that he wouldn't get to compete in the finals. But she barely thought about that as Noah was surrounded by the others.

"Congrats, dude!" Mackenzie exclaimed, dancing around like a jumping bean. "This is so amazing!"

Everyone except Ty swarmed around Noah, chattering excitedly about the finals. Izzy stood back and watched Noah, more curious than ever now. What was the deal with him, anyway?

Nineteen

MACKENZIE LEANED FORWARD eagerly as the *JNC* theme music started to play on the big Fit Kidz TV set. "Ready to be a star, Noah?" It was a week and a half after the wildcard taping, and Noah's episode was about to air. "Actually," Mackenzie added with a grin, "I guess you're used to being a star already, huh?"

"Quiet, Mack," Izzy ordered before Noah could respond. "It's starting, and I want to hear the show, not you — okay?"

Mackenzie laughed, knowing that Izzy was just kidding around. The older girl had seemed kind of prickly at first, but now Mackenzie really liked her.

"Make room for Momma!" a loud voice cried out.

Mackenzie giggled as Mrs. Perry-Dhawan — "Call me

Stella, please!" she'd ordered everyone when she'd arrived —rushed forward. JJ scooted over so she could sit beside her son.

"This is so exciting!" Stella said, grabbing Noah around the shoulders and squeezing him. "My baby, on national TV!"

"Mom, shhh," Noah said. "People want to hear."

"Oh, don't be silly," his mother said. "People will forgive me for being a proud mother!"

Mackenzie smiled, then looked around the gym. About two dozen people had gathered to watch the wildcard show on TV, with Noah and his parents as the guests of honor. Mr. Dhawan was near the back of the group, where he'd been chatting with Daddy Jim about science.

Onscreen, Mellie Monroe was explaining about the wildcard contest. "At the end of today's show, the fate of our alternates will be decided," she declared. "We'll just have to wait and see how many of our wildcard ninjas make the cut!"

"No, we won't," Ty muttered.

"Shhh!" Mackenzie warned, glancing around again. She knew Ty was disappointed that ten ninjas had made it in from the wildcard group. It meant he was less likely to be called in to compete in the finals, though there was still a chance if someone got sick or something. But most of the people in the gym hadn't been at the wildcard taping, so they didn't know the results yet. Mackenzie didn't want Ty to accidentally ruin the suspense.

The show was just as exciting as all the others. Noah's turn came near the middle. Everyone cheered when he appeared onscreen, and Stella stood up and whistled loudly.

"Go, baby, go!" she cheered. "Hey, when did you film this?"

Noah's package was starting. It showed him with his father at home. There was also a scene at a dance studio and a few at Fit Kidz.

When it finished, everyone applauded. But Stella turned to Noah, looking confused. "Where was I when the camera crew came to our house?" she asked.

Noah kept staring at the TV. "Um, they had to do it that day you were at your school reunion," he said quickly. "I thought we told you."

"No, you didn't." Noah's mother still sounded confused, but Mackenzie didn't have time to wonder what was going on. On TV, Noah was starting his round.

"Well, that was fun," Mr. Dhawan said as the final credits rolled. Noah's father was a tall, thin man who always seemed to be smiling. "Thanks for inviting us."

"Wait, we're not leaving yet, are we?" Stella said. "I want to see the ninja room."

"Mom, the gym is technically closed," Noah protested. "We can't—"

"No, it's okay, Noah," Mrs. Santiago said. "Go ahead and give your parents a tour if you like."

Mackenzie followed as Noah and his parents headed to the ninja room. So did Tara, Izzy, JJ, and Kevin, though Ty stayed behind in the main room.

Stella oohed and aahed over all the obstacles, especially the Crazy Cliff. "It's so tall!" she exclaimed. "How did you ever make it all the way up that thing, Noah?"

"Strong legs," Mr. Dhawan put in with a smile. "Thanks to all those dance classes."

Tara chuckled. "It seems really high at first, but you get used to it," she told Stella.

"Maybe you youngsters do, but it scares me!" Stella declared with a dramatic shudder. She pointed to the balance beam. "That, on the other hand, looks like fun. Can I try?"

"Mom, no!" Noah looked horrified.

But Tara laughed. "Go ahead," she said. "Just be careful."

"Don't worry. In the theater, we like to tell each other to break a leg." Stella winked broadly. "But we don't like to actually do it!"

For the next few minutes Stella tried out the beam, the rings, and even the Loco Ladder, though she gave up after missing the first hole three times, laughing as she tumbled to the mat. Everyone else laughed, too—Stella was hilarious!

"Okay. Clearly my son is more talented than his old mum," she said. "And never fear, stalwart fans—*Junior Ninja Champion* won't be Noah's last star turn. You should all come out and see him starring in *Beauty and the Beast* this fall!"

"Mom, stop," Noah protested.

"Hush. Don't be modest." Stella flapped her hands at him. "You know you're going to land the part of Chip." She grinned. "But guess what? I'm thinking of making my own return to acting by auditioning for the part of Mrs. Potts! Won't that be fun? Mother and son, acting together."

Mackenzie nodded and applauded. She'd seen *Beauty and the Beast* lots of times, and she was sure the mother-son pair would have a blast acting together in the show.

She glanced at Noah to see what he thought. But he was staring at his feet, not even smiling. Weird! Mackenzie wanted to go over and ask what was wrong, but just then Mr. Dhawan announced that it was time to go and bustled his wife and son out of the room.

Twenty

NOAH WAS FUMING by the time he and his parents got home. His mother had spent most of the short car ride discussing the trip out to L.A. for the finals. But as they walked into the house, she started babbling about those auditions again.

". . . and we can get you in for a few extra vocal lessons with Andre," she said. "You'll want to make sure you're ready to wow the audition committee." She smiled and winked. "Although the publicity from this ninja show can't hurt your chances, eh? Everybody loves a winner." She started humming a song from an old movie musical with that line in it.

But Noah had finally had enough. "Stop!" he cried,

tossing his gym bag aside so hard that it slid under a chair in the front hallway. "Mom, just stop, okay? I don't want that stupid part!"

"What?" His mother blinked at him, looking startled. "Of course you do."

Noah clenched his fists at his sides to stop his hands from trembling. He felt a little bit sick to his stomach, and for a second he was tempted to take it back. He could say he was joking, change the subject . . .

But if he did that, nothing would change. And wasn't that why he'd started this whole ninja thing? To try to change things, to turn his life into what he'd visualized it could be like?

"No, I don't," he said, following his mother, who was already heading into the kitchen. "I hate having to act and sing solos! Why won't you just let me dance? That's what I'm good at — it's what I like!"

"You're good at everything!" Stella exclaimed. "Don't sell yourself short! I know you'd love singing and acting if you gave it more of a chance. That's why I think this Chip part would be so wonderful for you. All it will take is hard work — and look at how hard you've worked at this ninja thing! You could do the same with the show!"

"But that's the whole reason I worked so hard to become a ninja," Noah blurted, unable to hold in the truth anymore. "I thought I could become a TV star that way, and that would finally make you happy."

His mother's jaw dropped. For a second she didn't say anything.

"Stella?" Noah's father said softly. He'd followed them into the kitchen without Noah's noticing. "You okay?"

"No," Noah's mom said. "I'm utterly and completely shocked and dismayed."

Noah winced. He should have known this crazy plan wouldn't work.

Noah's mother clutched the back of a chair, still looking distraught. "Noah, I had no idea you felt this way! I thought you loved the theater as much as I do!"

"I do, Mom," Noah said. "But only the dancing part."

"I always said you were pushing him too hard, Stella," Noah's dad chided gently. "You can't force him to have the same dreams you had at his age."

"I suppose not." Noah's mother looked sad for a moment. Then she turned to face Noah. "So what do you want to do? Quit the theater?"

"No, not quit completely," Noah said. "But, um, maybe I could drop out of voice and acting lessons?"

"Oh, baby . . ." Noah's mom began.

"Stella . . ." his dad said.

She sighed. "Okay, it's a deal. You still want to dance, though, don't you?"

"Of course. I love dancing—I definitely still want to do that." Noah shrugged. "I want to keep doing ninja stuff, too."

His mother looked surprised. "You still want to be a ninja?" she asked. "But you said you only did it for me."

"I did." A smile spread across Noah's face as he realized something for the first time. "At first. But now I love it almost as much as dancing!"

Twenty-One

TY RAISED THE WEIGHT on the leg press, then flopped onto the bench. Across the room, his teammates were already gathered around the TV.

"Ty, come on!" JJ called. "It's going to start in a minute."

"Then I'll be there in a minute," Ty called back as he lifted steadily — one, two, one, two . . .

Mackenzie didn't seem satisfied by his response. She hurried over and poked Ty in the shoulder.

"Come on," she said. "It's the last semis show! You don't want to miss a second, right?"

"I guess." Ty did a few more reps, then lowered the bar and stood. "I just want to make sure I'm ready when they call me in at the finals." For the past couple of weeks, ever since the wildcard show had aired, Ty had been working harder than ever. Okay, so maybe ten ninjas had qualified from the wildcard show, but an alternate was still an alternate, right? And he'd overheard Mackenzie and Noah talking about visualizing how they wanted stuff to happen. Ty could totally visualize himself stepping in at the last minute — and triumphing!

"All it would take is another busted ankle, like the kid who had to drop out when JJ got in," he told Mackenzie as they headed back across the gym. "Or maybe someone getting sick or missing their flight . . ."

Mackenzie looked dismayed. "Don't say that stuff!" she exclaimed. "It's like you're wishing bad luck on other people. That's not nice."

Ty just shrugged. He wasn't wishing bad luck on anyone. Just good luck on himself. But he figured Mackenzie wouldn't understand. She didn't even seem to care about not making the finals.

The show was fun to watch, as always. But this time Ty was more focused on the details. He watched all the competitors carefully, especially the ones who did well. He wanted to be ready to beat all of them.

During the commercial breaks he watched his teammates — especially Izzy, JJ, and Noah. He needed to be ready to beat them, too.

But I'm not wishing them bad luck, he told himself with a glance toward Mackenzie. *I'd be really happy if they came in second, third, and fourth. Just as long as I'm number one!*

Twenty-Two

"YOU SHOULD TAKE THIS, sweetie!" Izzy's stepmonster, Tina, had been digging through Izzy's closet. She held up a flowered dress that Izzy hadn't even seen in several years. "We might want to go out for a nice dinner or something while we're in L.A."

"That doesn't fit me anymore." Izzy tossed two more pairs of gym socks into her suitcase. "Anyway, we probably won't have time for stuff like that."

"Sure we will," said her older sister, Hannah, who was lounging on the end of the bed. "We don't fly back until Wednesday, remember?"

"Whatever." Izzy frowned at both of them. "I can pack

my own bag, okay? But it would be a lot easier without all kinds of extra people in my room."

"Oh, dear." Tina winked at Hannah. "Sounds like that's our cue to leave."

Hannah pushed herself to her feet. "Yeah, okay, Ms. I'm-Cranky-Cuz-I'm-Nervous-but-I-Won't-Admit-It. We're out of here."

To Izzy's relief, the two of them headed out the door. She was nervous, all right, but not because of *JNC*. Not that she was about to tell those two the real reason.

As Izzy pulled some T-shirts out of her dresser, Tina poked her head back in. "Don't forget that California's in a different time zone," she said. "You'd better go to bed a little early so you're well rested."

Izzy grimaced as her stepmother disappeared. She'd forgotten all about the time difference! It made her even more anxious about what to do about that party, which was due to start in a couple of hours.

Maybe I can just go for a little while, she told herself. *I can make sure I'm home by midnight, then nap on the plane tomorrow . . .*

She jumped as something scratched against her window. When she hurried over, she saw Jess perched on the peak of the garage roof just outside.

Izzy threw open the window. "How'd you get up there?" she hissed, shooting a look behind her to make sure her sister and stepmother were really gone and her door was closed.

"How else?" Jess grinned and vaulted in through the window. "Parkour."

Izzy nodded. That was how she and Jess had become friends — they were both into parkour, which was all about running, jumping, and climbing. Of course Jess wouldn't think twice about scaling the rose arbor and then running along the roof peak to Izzy's second-story window.

"What are you doing here?" Izzy asked in a low voice, hoping nobody could hear them. "The party doesn't start for hours."

"Duh." Jess wandered toward the closet, which Tina had left standing open. "Just came by to see what you're planning to wear tonight. And help with your hair and makeup." She shrugged. "Just 'cause you'll probably be the youngest one there, you don't have to look like it, right?"

Izzy nodded, relieved that Jess was back to acting friendly. Maybe this was her way of saying she was sorry for being so distant lately.

But she hasn't actually said she's sorry, Izzy thought, her happiness fading as quickly as it had come. *I mean, she totally ghosted my premiere party and pretty much the whole ninja thing . . .*

So maybe it was time to find out where their friendship really stood. "Listen," she said. "I might have to bail on the party tonight."

"What?" Jess's smile disappeared instantly. "You're kidding, right?"

Izzy shrugged. "Nope. I have a really early flight tomorrow."

"So what? You can sleep when you're dead." Jess laughed, but it sounded a little forced. "Nobody skips this party. Nobody."

"Okay," Izzy said. "But there's all kinds of events for us ninjas when we get to California tomorrow, and then I have to be at the competition bright and early on Sunday morning. With the time change and everything, I just thought . . ."

Her voice trailed off. Jess's expression had gone hard and cold. "Maybe you should think again," she said. "Because no friend of mine would ever bail on me like that."

"Yeah." Izzy swallowed hard. "I hear you, Jess. Loud and clear."

"Good. So you're going, right?"

Izzy hesitated, not sure for a second what she was going to say. She thought about all the fun she'd had with Jess over the past year or so. Was she really ready to give that up?

"Sorry," she told Jess before she could lose her nerve. "If you'd bounce me for something like that, maybe we were never really friends to start with."

The older girl's eyes widened in surprise, then narrowed. "You can't be serious."

"Yeah, I am." Izzy waved toward the window. "You'd better leave, Jess."

Jess just glared at her for a second. Then she stormed

over to the window, vaulted through, and disappeared into the darkness outside.

Izzy collapsed on her messy bed, wondering if she'd just made a huge mistake. Just then her phone buzzed.

When she grabbed it off the bedside table, Izzy saw that it was a text from Mackenzie:

> Check it out, Iz! I made T-shirts for the rest of us to wear while we watch u compete. Cool, right? It was supposed to be a surprise, but Ty is saying he won't wear it so u need to help me convince him . . .

By the time she scrolled down to the attached photo, Izzy was smiling. There were Mackenzie and Kevin, goofy grins on their faces, posing in bright neon yellow shirts with the words FIT KIDZ 4EVA! printed on them.

"Mack, you're such a nut," she muttered.

But she was still smiling. And feeling pretty good again despite what had just happened with Jess.

Who needed fake friends like her, anyway? Izzy already had the real thing.

Twenty-Three

JJ TOOK A DEEP BREATH, glancing down at the sliver of space showing between the end of the gangplank and the doorway into the plane. Then he stepped through, clutching his carry-on bag.

"Whoo, JJ!" Mackenzie rushed on behind him. "It's your first time on a plane, right?"

"Yeah." JJ felt a little nervous, but excited, too. "So now what?"

"Now we sit." Izzy glanced back at him over her shoulder. "Come on. I think I'm supposed to have the window seat, but we can switch if you want."

"Cool, thanks," JJ said, following Izzy down the narrow aisle. His parents were on this flight, too, along with most of the other families. But the Santiagos had arranged for all the kids to sit together.

Ty was already seated in the row behind JJ, Izzy, and Noah. He stood up and clapped JJ on the shoulder as he took his seat.

"Ready to soar through the sky, bro?" he asked.

"Ready as I'll ever be." JJ was glad that Ty was in a good mood. He still wasn't being very friendly to Noah, but other than that, he was almost back to normal.

JJ clutched the armrests when the engines roared to life and again when he felt the plane's wheels leave the runway, but once they were in the air, he forgot all about being nervous. The sun had just risen, and he could see half the state spread out beneath him.

"I think I see our town!" he cried, pressing his nose against the plastic window.

"Can you see Fit Kidz down there?" Mackenzie asked with a laugh. "Make sure the Santiagos remembered to turn off the lights!"

Everyone in both rows laughed, including JJ. A few minutes later the plane had climbed high enough for the clouds to block his view.

But that was okay. He and his teammates had plenty to talk about!

Twenty-Four

WOW!" MACKENZIE STOPPED on the sidewalk between the taxi stand and the hotel, staring up at the tall palm trees towering over the street. "California is like a whole different world!"

Daddy Jim poked her in the back. "Keep moving, Mack," he said. "We're running late, and you don't want to miss the welcome luncheon."

That sent Mackenzie scurrying forward into the cool glass lobby of the hotel. JJ and his family were already there, signing in.

"This is amazing, huh?" JJ told Mackenzie. "I never thought I'd stay in a hotel like this."

"Me either," Mackenzie said. "I wonder where our

lunch is going to be." She'd memorized the weekend's schedule. Today all the competing ninjas and their coaches were invited to a luncheon at the hotel. Each of them was allowed two guests, and Tara was bringing Mackenzie and Kevin. JJ's mother had offered to go sightseeing with Jasmine and Mackenzie's dads instead of attending, so that Ty could take her spot.

After that, they were free to rest, work out at the hotel gym, or sightsee in Los Angeles. The competition would begin bright and early on Sunday morning and finish on Labor Day, which was Monday.

JJ's mom was digging through her bag, but she looked up at Mackenzie's words. "Why don't you kids go ahead with Tara and find out where it's being held?" she suggested. "We can unpack without you."

"Agreed," Papa Kurt said, walking over. "Tara's waiting for you over there."

Mackenzie looked to where he was pointing. Tara was waiting near a doorway that was labeled as the ballroom.

"Let's go," Mackenzie said, and JJ nodded.

A few minutes later the whole team walked into the ballroom together. It was a huge room, with a buffet set up at one end and tables and chairs at the other. In the middle, tons of kids and adults were milling around, talking.

"Check it out." Izzy elbowed Mackenzie. "Isn't that the Mighty Mini over there?"

Mackenzie pushed her glasses up her nose so she could

see better. "Yeah, it's totally her!" she exclaimed. "Wow, she looks even tinier in person."

"Didn't that guy compete in our semis?" Ty asked, pointing toward a red-haired kid nearby.

Mackenzie recognized him right away. "Yeah, his name's Vince. He did really well."

"Oh wow, and there's Stretch McKenzie!" Kevin exclaimed. "He was on *NNC* last season with Tara, remember? I heard he's coaching a team from Philadelphia."

"He is," Tara said, smiling and waving at the other adult ninja. "I think I'll go say hi. You kids go ahead and mingle, okay? I'll meet you at our table later."

Mackenzie nodded and threw herself into the crowd. There were so many interesting people here! She couldn't wait to meet them all.

"So everyone is talking about which ninjas are the ones to beat," Izzy said.

Mackenzie and the others had been at the luncheon for a little over an hour. A few minutes earlier, Mellie Monroe had arrived and told everyone it was time to sit down and eat. She was supposed to make some announcements in a little while.

Kevin took a sip of water. "Yeah, and everyone says the same thing. Chen the Mighty Mini and Benny the Beast."

"And JJ and Izzy and Noah," Mackenzie put in loyally.

Izzy snorted. "Not really," she said. "But that's okay. We can sneak up and beat them anyway, right?"

She traded a high-five with JJ, and Noah smiled. "Don't forget me," Ty said. "Once I get called in, I bet everyone will add me to the list."

Tara looked concerned. "Ty, it's good that you're ready to go if needed," she said. "But I hope you're not—"

"Look!" Kevin blurted out, cutting off whatever the coach was going to say. "Here comes Benny the Beast!"

"Really?" Mackenzie spun around in her seat. "Benny! Yo, Benny! Over here!"

Benny walked toward her, looking a little confused. "Hi. Do I know you?"

Mackenzie grinned at him. "No, but I know you. You were amazing in semis! Can I have your autograph?"

"Um, sure." While Mackenzie searched for something for him to sign, Benny glanced at Ty. "I remember you. Tough break on the cliff, dude."

"Yeah." Ty shrugged. "It's cool, I'll kill it next time."

Benny nodded and grinned. "Well, I'm planning to kill it this time," he said, glancing around at Izzy, JJ, and Noah. "Sorry to tell you guys, but this competition is mine."

"Oh yeah?" Izzy said. "We'll see about that."

"Yeah," Benny said, grabbing the napkin Mackenzie was handing him. "We will."

"Attention! May I have your attention please?" Mellie

Monroe was at the main table with a microphone. "Please take your seats so we can explain how the weekend's schedule will work."

"Thanks," Mackenzie whispered as Benny quickly scrawled his name on the napkin and then hurried off to his own table. She leaned back in her seat, hardly daring to believe she was really here, in California, getting ready to watch her teammates compete in the morning. This was amazing!

Twenty-Five

"WOW." JJ SWALLOWED HARD as he looked up—up—up at the framework of the finals course on Sunday morning. "This looks way bigger than the semis!"

"Of course it does." Kevin was studying a large TV camera hanging nearby. "This is the big time, right?"

Mackenzie pumped her fist. "Whoo-hoo!"

JJ hardly heard her. He shaded his eyes against the bright California sunshine as he surveyed the huge, colorful course. It was set up in a park in the middle of the city. A large canvas tent was nearby—where competitors could warm up or get out of the sun when they weren't competing. A large crowd had already gathered in the spectator area, even though the taping wasn't going to start for a couple of hours.

"Look," Noah said. "The Crazy Cliff is in the middle of the course instead of at the end!"

Kevin nodded. "That happens on the adult show, too."

"Yeah," Ty put in. "The last obstacle is usually something even scarier."

Tara checked her watch. "The demo should start soon," she said. "Pay attention, and we'll talk about it afterward while we walk the course."

JJ nodded. A moment later a production assistant announced that the demonstration was about to begin. Then a teenage boy stepped onto the start mat.

"He must be at least sixteen," Izzy commented. "That doesn't seem fair. He'll probably make it seem easier than it is."

JJ didn't say anything. He wasn't sure anybody could make that course look easy.

He watched with the rest as the demonstration ninja went through the course, showing the competitors how each obstacle was supposed to be completed. First came a set of balance steps called Stepping Out, just like in the semis — except this time there were six steps instead of five. Next was a rope obstacle called Monkey Business, then several others. JJ was so nervous he was having trouble focusing. He watched the demo ninja race up the Crazy Cliff, which was sixth on the course. Then came three more obstacles, and finally the tenth and final one, which was called the Wall Crawl.

"Whoa," JJ whispered as the demo ninja did it. The Wall Crawl consisted of two sheer walls set just a little less than arm's length apart, with crabs and other scuttling creatures painted all over them. The ninja had to "crab-walk" up by pressing his arms and legs against the walls and moving them up a little at a time.

"That looks super hard." Izzy said. She had gone a little pale as she watched the demo.

JJ just nodded. They hadn't practiced anything like that back at Fit Kidz!

When the demonstration was over, Tara led the whole team into the alley beside the course, where each competitor's family and friends were allowed to stand while the ninja competed. She stopped beside each obstacle, giving tips on how to attack it. But JJ hardly heard her. He kept being distracted by the spectators, who were making a lot of noise, and the course, which looked even bigger up close, and the cameras, which seemed to be everywhere. This was overwhelming! Suddenly he couldn't help remembering how nice it had been to be ordinary, just hanging out in his tree house without having to worry about acting like a celebrity or being on TV or messing up in front of so many people . . .

They were at the seventh obstacle, a set of balance balls called Round and Round, when Noah elbowed JJ. "You okay?" he whispered. "You seem a little out of it."

"Yeah," JJ whispered back. "Um, guess I've got a touch of stage fright."

That was what Mackenzie had called it at semifinals. JJ wasn't sure Noah would know what he was talking about, but Noah nodded.

"I get that too," Noah said. "Before every performance. You just have to get past it."

"How?" JJ glanced toward the audience, then toward Tara, who was demonstrating something for Izzy. "This is nuts!"

"Deep breathing sometimes helps me focus," Noah said. "Also, try to picture yourself doing everything perfectly. Don't even think about what might go wrong." He smiled. "Then just remind yourself that you love doing this."

JJ smiled back, suddenly very glad that Noah was on the team. "Thanks. I'll try it."

Twenty-Six

"THEY SHOULD BE BACK SOON," Ty muttered, pacing back and forth in the warm-up area.

The course walk had ended a few minutes earlier. Now the entire team was drinking water and waiting for Ty's parents, who had gone to find out the run order for the two days of competition.

Which means they'll also find out if the alternates are getting called in, Ty thought, flexing his biceps as he walked. *I know I'm going to get my chance to compete—I have to!*

Mackenzie pointed. "There they are!"

Ty's mother was shuffling through some papers when she and Ty's dad reached the group. "Okay, we've got some interesting news," she said.

Ty held his breath, sure that his mom was going to tell him he was in.

But instead, she pointed to Izzy. "You're going first," she said. "Not just of our group, I mean — first in the whole competition."

"Really?" Izzy gulped. "Um, okay."

Mr. Santiago glanced at Noah. "You're going today, too," he told him. "Not until this afternoon, though."

"That's good," Tara said. "It's easier if we're spaced out."

Ty's mom nodded. "JJ, you don't compete until tomorrow," she said. "Your turn should come toward the end of the day."

"Great." JJ grinned. "That gives me even more time to get nervous."

Noah laughed. "Or more time to picture perfection," he said.

But Ty wasn't paying attention to the two of them. "Well?" he said impatiently. "What about me?"

His dad glanced at him and cleared his throat. "I'm sorry, son. Everyone showed up, so they won't need any alternates."

Ty didn't respond — he couldn't. It felt as if his entire world had just come crashing down. He'd been so sure . . .

"Sorry, Ty," Kevin said.

"Yeah," Mackenzie added. "You'll get 'em next year."

Ty's mother didn't say anything. But she reached over and squeezed his shoulder.

Ty took a deep breath. "Um, thanks, guys."

He shook off his mother's hand and walked away, needing some space to deal with this. He watched from a distance as the rest of the group dispersed, with Izzy, JJ, and Kevin heading to the cooler to get more water and Mackenzie walking over to take photos of the course. Meanwhile, Noah wandered off by himself and sat down. He started rubbing his left ankle, grimacing.

Ty's heart thumped. *Hold on,* he thought, hope flaring inside him. *Maybe there's still a chance.*

He rushed over to Noah. "What's wrong?" he demanded. "Are you injured? If you are, you should tell someone right away so the alternate has time to get warmed up."

Twenty-Seven

NOAH WAS STARTLED when Ty suddenly rushed over and got in his face, yelling something about injuries and alternates. But after a second, he got it.

"Sorry," he said quickly. "I'm not hurt or anything. It's just an old dance injury that gets a little sore sometimes — no big deal. I'm definitely not dropping out."

Ty's face fell. Noah braced himself, guessing that Ty might snarl at him or something. It was pretty obvious that he resented that Noah was competing and he wasn't. Actually, it seemed like he just resented Noah — period.

But Ty took a deep breath. "Okay, whatever," he said. "I mean, it's cool that you can work through some pain. I had a hamstring injury last soccer season, but I still started every game. I just powered through it."

"Yeah." Noah tried not to let his surprise show. Ty was actually being . . . nice! "I know what you mean. Even if my ankle is killing me, I can't let the audience see that I'm sore."

Ty laughed. "You can't let the opposing team see it, either. Otherwise they'll tear you apart."

Noah smiled. "Listen, Ty . . ." He paused, not sure he should say what he was thinking. But maybe it was better to be honest, the way he'd been with his mom. "Um, I'm sorry you didn't make the finals. And if it's my fault in any way, you know—"

"It's not," Ty broke in. "You did your thing, and I did mine. I just didn't make the cut this year, that's all." He shrugged, then grinned. "But next year, look out! I'm not only planning on making the finals—I'm planning on winning!"

Noah smiled. "Cool."

"Yeah." Ty shrugged again. "But in the meantime, I'm hoping one of my teammates will bring home the championship. You know—keep it in the family."

Noah nodded, glancing toward the rest of the group. "JJ's really strong," he said. "And Izzy's amazing—she could win the whole thing if she has a good run."

"Yeah. And so could you." Ty clapped him on the shoulder. "You're on this team too, you know."

For the first time, Noah felt as if that really might be true. It was a nice feeling.

"Thanks," he said, shooting Ty an uncertain glance. "Since we're on the same team, I have a favor to ask."

Ty looked a little surprised, but he nodded. "Sure. What?"

"I was, um, whispering with JJ for part of the course walk." Noah grinned sheepishly. "Want to give me some tips on a few of the tougher obstacles so I don't have to admit that to Tara?"

Twenty-Eight

*B*REATHE, IZZY TOLD HERSELF as she bounced from one foot to the other on the start mat. *Don't forget to breathe.*

She wasn't sure she'd ever been so nervous and jittery in her life. But she was excited, too. Okay, so going first wasn't ideal, since she wouldn't get to see how the course was running. On the other hand, she couldn't wait to try some of the new obstacles!

Mellie Monroe was talking to the camera. Izzy couldn't hear her very well over the noise of the crowd, but it didn't matter. She'd catch that stuff later on TV. Right now she kept one eye on the first obstacle, Stepping Out, and another on the production assistant who was supposed to tell her when to start.

Izzy mopped her brow with the back of one hand. It was a hot day, made even hotter by all the TV lights. But she wasn't really thinking about that.

"Whenever you're ready, ninja," the PA said.

A buzzer sounded, and Izzy took off, skipping easily through all six balance steps. She could hear the crowd going wild, and she knew she'd just laid down a time for the rest of the competitors to beat. But she was already focusing on the second obstacle, Monkey Business. Mackenzie had said it was similar to a ropes obstacle Noah had faced in his tryouts, which made Izzy wish she'd gone to see him.

But whatever — she'd seen the demo ninja do it, so she knew how it worked. She had to climb a long rope and then swing through a series of shorter ones. Tara had warned that the dismount might be the hardest part, since it was a pretty good jump from the final rope. If Izzy missed and fell into the net instead, she'd be disqualified.

But no worries, she thought, flexing her hands as she caught her breath. *It's no harder than climbing the drainpipe to Jess's room, and I've done that a million times.*

She felt a flash of sadness at the thought of her friend, or ex-friend, or whatever Jess was. But she pushed it aside, putting all her focus into what she was doing as she grabbed the rope.

Izzy's arms were tired by the time she made it through

Monkey Business and a set of stationary bars called Bar None. She was glad that a balance obstacle came next. It was called Touch and Go. Ninjas had to skip across a series of blocks without knocking over a bunch of vases and stuff that were perched precariously on extra blocks in between. It looked like it was tricky but fun — like jumping a flower garden on her skateboard without damaging anything.

Izzy grinned when she landed on the mat at the end of the obstacle. That had been fun! Four down, six to go . . .

The fifth obstacle was the Loco Ladder. That had always been a tough one for Izzy, especially since she sometimes got nervous near the top, due to her fear of heights. She couldn't help noticing that this particular Loco Ladder was a good four feet taller than the one from the semis.

But by the time she neared the top, she wasn't really thinking about the height. Just about her arm muscles, which were screaming as she wedged the right-hand peg into the second-to-last hole . . .

"Ugh!" she cried as she felt her left hand slip. She scrabbled for a better grip, but it was too late — she tucked and rolled as she fell down, down, down into the safety net.

"Good try, Izzy!" Mellie Monroe cried on the loudspeaker. "You almost made it to the top."

Izzy forced herself to smile and wave to the crowd, which was roaring with applause. Where was her family? She hadn't thought to look for them before she started, so she didn't know if anyone had told them they could come down to the alley for her run. This was their first time seeing her do her thing in person, though of course they'd watched her episode on TV. Would they be disappointed that she hadn't done better? Would it make them think that this whole ninja thing was pointless, that she should go back to running, like them?

"Izzy! Yo, Iz!" a familiar voice cut through the chaos.

It was Izzy's older brother, Charlie. He was grinning and pumping his fists as he ran toward her. Izzy's sister, father, and stepmother were right behind him.

"Wow!" Hannah skidded to a stop in front of Izzy, breathless. "I had no idea you could do stuff like that! I mean, I saw you on TV before, but this was different."

"Yeah." Izzy's father enfolded her in a huge hug. "I'm so proud of you, Isabella."

All four of them started asking all kinds of questions about the course and about being a ninja. But Izzy was too stunned and out of breath to answer at first.

Luckily, her teammates appeared just in time. "That last thing is called the Loco Ladder," Mackenzie told Izzy's family, pointing up. "It's super hard! You need to be really strong, and also really careful . . ."

With that, she was off and running, talking a mile a minute the way she always did. Ty and Kevin added some comments, too. JJ and Noah didn't say much, but they nodded and smiled.

"I know Izzy went first, so you don't have much to

compare her to," Kevin put in. "But she'll probably have one of the best performances through the balance things."

JJ nodded. "She's better than any of us at balance stuff."

"Hey." Ty frowned. "Speak for yourself." Then he grinned. "But yeah, he's right. Izzy's a beast on balance obstacles."

Izzy felt herself blushing as her family stared at her, looking impressed. "Thanks, guys," she said. "I wish I'd made it farther. But wow, that was cool!"

Twenty-Nine

I THINK THAT CAMERA'S pointing at us!" Mackenzie poked Kevin in the arm, excitement surging through her. "Quick! Wave! Maybe they'll show our T-shirts on TV!"

She jumped up and down, waving and whooping. Beside her, Kevin did the same thing. Mackenzie could see her dads out of the corner of her eye. They were in the bleachers a little ways back from where she and the others were watching.

She glanced around for Ty, wondering if he was still wearing the shirt she'd made for him. But he was too far away to notice her. He and Noah were watching together as a ninja struggled through the bar obstacle.

She stopped jumping when the camera turned away. "That's weird," she said.

"What?" Kevin asked.

"Ty and Noah are hanging out together all of a sudden." Mackenzie squinted at the pair, curious.

Then she shrugged, figuring it didn't matter what had happened. She was having a great time, and she was glad that all her teammates were, too. It was amazing to be at the finals! She was taking lots of pictures for her blog and trying to remember everything so she could write about it later. She wouldn't be able to give away what had happened until the show aired next week, of course — everyone there had signed a paper saying that. But she could write it all out now and post it later. She couldn't wait!

"Uh-oh!" Kevin's voice interrupted her thoughts. "He almost hit the first vase."

The ninja on course had just started Touch and Go. Mackenzie groaned along with everyone else when he knocked over the second vase and was eliminated.

Izzy rushed over. "The Mighty Mini goes next," she reported. "Let's get closer."

Mackenzie nodded, eager to see if Chen did as well as she had at semis. She followed as Izzy wriggled her way past some adults to the ropes that separated the spectators from the course.

"There she goes," Kevin said as Chen leaped onto the

first step of Stepping Out. "Where's JJ? He should be watching his competition."

"I think he went up to say hi to his family, since he's not running until tomorrow." Mackenzie didn't take her eyes off Chen, who was already moving on to Monkey Business.

By the time the Mighty Mini raced up the Crazy Cliff and immediately slid down the far side to attack the next obstacle, Mackenzie was holding her breath. Chen was amazing! Mackenzie still wanted one of her teammates to win, but she couldn't help cheering as the Mighty Mini danced across the next balance obstacle and reached Door to Door, in which ninjas had to swing and jump through a course consisting of several door frames hung at different heights.

After that, there was just one more obstacle to go, and once Chen finished it, she was facing the Wall Crawl.

"She's so short, I wonder if her arms and legs will even reach the walls," Mackenzie said, holding her breath as she watched.

She didn't have to hold it for long. Chen almost had to do a split, and her arms were stretched out nearly straight — but she crab-walked up the wall without hesitation!

"Oh my gosh! She did it!" Izzy cried. "She finished!"

"That was incredible! And so fast," Kevin added. "Go, Mighty Mini!"

The crowd was going wild, just as they'd done at the

wildcard show. Mackenzie hurried over to Ty and Noah, who had been watching nearby.

"Look out, Dancing Ninja," she told Noah with a grin. "That time is going to be hard to beat!"

Thirty

NOAH WAS FEELING confident as he stepped onto the start mat. He waved to his parents and teammates, who were all standing together in the viewing alley. Then he turned to watch the big screen beside the course as his package started to play.

All the finalists had filmed new packages, since the producers didn't want to show the exact same videos that viewers had already seen in the semis. This time Noah had told his mother about it. He'd been afraid she might try to take over, maybe make the whole thing about his future Broadway career or something. But she seemed to have taken their talk to heart. True, she'd fussed with his hair forever and kept gesturing for him to smile, but she'd mostly let Noah and the producers decide what to include. Because of that, the package felt like the real Noah.

I hope Mom notices that this is the real me, too, he thought as the final shot focused in on him powering up the Fit Kidz climbing wall. *Not the me she's been imagining all these years. I think she's finally starting to get it.*

He shot a look toward his parents, who smiled and waved. Then the PA told him he could begin, and Noah immediately turned all his focus onto the course in front of him.

Stepping Out and Monkey Business went smoothly. Bar None was a little trickier—the bars didn't move at all, and Noah was surprised by how far apart they really were once he was up there. But he called upon his trapeze experience again and made it safely to the landing mat.

Next came Touch and Go, which was actually fun. Skipping across from block to block, jumping a little higher when there was a vase in the way—it reminded Noah of some choreography he'd done in his jazz class a year or two ago. The boys in the number had had to jump over the girls, and the girls were sure to threaten the boys with horrible things if they landed on any part of their bodies!

After that, this is a piece of cake, Noah told himself with a secret smile.

Then he got serious again because the Loco Ladder came next. He took a few deep breaths, pausing on the mat to make sure he was ready. One of the pegs missed its mark halfway up, but he managed to recover without losing his grip, shoving it in on the second try. Before he knew it, he was at the top!

"Climb that Cliff! Climb that Cliff!" the crowd chanted as Noah approached the next obstacle. He barely hesitated, pushing off into a run. Both hands grabbed the lip, and he swung himself up.

"Go, Noah!" someone shrieked as he hopped down the steps on the far side of the wall — he was pretty sure it was Mackenzie, though he didn't look. He was studying the next obstacle, Round and Round. It was another balance obstacle, but it looked trickier than most, since the steps he had to leap across were round balls of varying sizes.

I can do this, he told himself. *It's just like hitting a mark onstage.*

He hit the first three balls just right. But the fourth one was smaller and set a little lower than the rest, and he landed on it crooked.

"Oooh!" the crowd moaned as Noah slipped, windmilling his arms but unable to stop himself from tumbling into the safety net.

For a second, Noah's heart clenched with disappointment. He glanced at the final three obstacles. He'd come so close . . .

Then he saw Ty waiting for him with a bottle of water at the edge of the course. That reminded him of his teammate's new, improved attitude about not making the finals.

Ty was determined to come back better and stronger next year — and so was Noah.

He climbed out of the net. "Thanks," he said, accepting the water Ty handed him.

"Good run, buddy," Ty said. "That ball thing looks brutal."

"Yeah." Noah grinned. "I'll be ready for it next year, though. Hope you are, too, if you want to have any chance of beating me."

"Oh, it's on," Ty said with a smirk. He raised his hand, and Noah laughed and gave him a high-five, glad that they were finally friends.

Thirty-One

"THIS IS FUN," Kevin said, reaching for another handful of pretzels. The whole team was hanging out in the hotel suite he shared with Ty and JJ. Most of them were sitting on the couch or the floor so they could reach the pizza and other snacks that the Santiagos had dropped off for them a little while ago. But Izzy was lounging in the chair by the window, sipping on a water and flipping through the channels on the TV.

"Hey, check it out!" she called suddenly, interrupting Mackenzie's chatter about the top contenders from the first day's competition. "We're on TV!"

"What?" Kevin hopped to his feet and hurried closer. The others followed.

The local news was on. A reporter was standing in front of a big sign with the *JNC* logo on it.

". . . and we're not even allowed to show our viewers a peek at the course," she said with a smile. "You'll have to wait until the show airs to see what devilish tests the producers have concocted for their young ninjas this time. I'll definitely be tuning in — I hope you all do, too!"

She said a few more words about how much local businesses were enjoying having the junior ninjas in town. But Kevin wasn't listening anymore.

"This is so cool!" he exclaimed. "I'm really glad my mom let me come."

Mackenzie stepped over and gave him a hug. "Me, too," she said. "It wouldn't be the same without the whole team here!"

JJ nodded. "I'll definitely need all of you cheering me on tomorrow," he said. "Otherwise I might die of nervousness."

"No, you won't." Ty laughed. "You're going to do great. Especially after Iz and Noah showed you how to do it. Right, guys?" He grinned at Izzy and slapped Noah on the back.

Kevin raised an eyebrow. He'd noticed that Ty and Noah seemed friendlier toward each other today. What had happened to change Ty's mind about the newest member of their team? Kevin had no idea, but he was glad.

When the news segment about the show ended, Izzy

yawned, clicked off the TV, and stood up. "I don't know about the rest of you, but I'm tired," she said. "We should all get to bed early so we're ready for tomorrow."

Kevin was a little disappointed that the party was breaking up. But he knew Izzy was right. JJ, especially, needed some rest.

"See you in the morning," he said. "I can't wait!"

Thirty-Two

TY WHOOPED AS VINCE, the red-haired kid from semis, raced up the Crazy Cliff. The final day of competition had been under way for a couple of hours, and Ty was having a great time. He still wished he could be competing himself, of course. But cheering his friends on was fun, too.

"Oh, no!" Mackenzie cried as Vince wiped out on the very first ball of Round and Round.

"That one looks really hard," JJ said, sounding nervous as he leaned on the metal fence that separated them from the course. "A lot of people are going down on those balls. Even Noah."

"You can do it." Ty clapped him on the back. "You're getting better at the balance stuff all the time."

JJ didn't say anything. Ty turned to watch the next ninja on course, a girl with freckles and wild, curly brown hair. She did pretty well, but fell on the Loco Ladder.

Mackenzie had grabbed a copy of the run order on the way in that morning. She consulted it, then gasped.

"Guess who's up next?" she said. "Benny the Beast!"

Sure enough, Benny stepped up to the start mat. He looked strong—he looked confident. Ty thought back to the luncheon on Saturday, when Benny had bragged about winning. But that was just trash talk. Lots of athletes did it, including Ty himself. It didn't mean that Benny was really as confident as he seemed.

"Maybe he'll choke," Ty said. "This is a lot of pressure. I bet he's super nervous."

"He doesn't look nervous," Izzy commented.

That was true. Benny smiled and waved to the crowd while his package played. Then he leaped onto the course, finishing the first few obstacles so fast that Ty barely had time to react as he watched.

"Wow, he's super speedy!" Mackenzie exclaimed.

"I wonder if he'll beat Chen's time," Noah added.

The Mighty Mini had had the fastest time so far. A couple of ninjas had come pretty close, but no one had been able to beat her.

Benny started scaling the Loco Ladder. "Did he just skip a level of holes?" Noah exclaimed.

"Yeah." Ty was amazed. He knew how hard that obstacle was even if you used all the holes. Benny was really strong if he could reach up and skip a level!

Benny had no trouble with the Crazy Cliff, and he sped through the next few obstacles as well. Before Ty knew it, Benny was powering up the Wall Crawl. When he reached the top, the whole place exploded in applause.

"Wow! Wow!" Mackenzie yelled. "That was amazing!"

Kevin was squinting at the timer. "He did it!" he cried. "He beat Chen by like four seconds!"

Ty noticed that JJ was the only one not cheering. His face was pale and he looked anxious.

"You okay?" Ty asked.

"Not really." JJ laughed, but it sounded weird. "I mean, should I even bother to take my turn? Some of these people are incredible! There's no way I can beat a performance like that." He glanced toward Benny, who had his arms raised in a victory dance atop the Wall Crawl.

"Are you kidding me?" Ty frowned at him. "You'd better not even think about dropping out!"

"Why not?" JJ stared at him. "If I do, maybe you can take my place."

For a split second Ty hesitated, thinking about that. *What if . . .*

But Mackenzie was already squealing with dismay. "No way!" she exclaimed. "JJ, you have to compete!"

"She's right," Ty said, knowing it was the right response even as he said it. "You made the finals. You earned this, you can totally do it. Don't psyche yourself out!"

"But . . ." JJ began.

"But nothing!" Ty poked him in the chest. "JJ, you're a great ninja. You're better on the climbing wall and the ropes than anyone — even me. Even Benny, I bet." He waved a hand toward the other ninja, who was finally climbing down from the last obstacle. "I want you to get out there and show us all how it's done!"

"Really?" JJ looked slightly less pale as he glanced at the course. "Yeah. Actually, I kind of want to try that ropes thing . . ."

"That's more like it!" Kevin said, sounding relieved. "Ty's right — you can do this, JJ!"

"Go, JJ!" Mackenzie cheered, pumping her fist.

Ty noticed that Benny was about to walk past them on his way to the locker room. He nodded. "Nice run, bro," Ty said.

"Thanks." Benny stopped, sounding a little out of breath, and glanced at JJ. "Yo, you haven't gone yet, have you?" When JJ shook his head, Benny added, "Be careful on that Door to Door thing. The second one doesn't swing as far as the first one — kinda threw me off for a sec."

"Got it. Thanks," JJ said. He raised his hand and fist bumped with Benny. "You looked great out there."

"Thanks." Benny grinned. "It was fun. Have a good trip — and may the best ninja win!"

"May the best ninja win," Ty chorused with JJ and the others.

Thirty-Three

"YOU'RE NEXT," TY TOLD JJ a couple of hours later.

JJ nodded, a wave of nervousness sweeping over him. "I know." He watched the ninja on course, who was rushing through Touch and Go. Two steps in, the guy crashed and fell, taking two or three vases with him, and JJ winced. "Everyone's trying to do the course so fast!"

"Blame Benny." Ty grinned. "Nobody's even come close to beating his time. You could do it, though!"

"Says who?" JJ shrugged. "You know me — nobody's ever going to tell me my nickname should be the Speedy Ninja."

That was true. Izzy had once joked that JJ should call himself the Tortoise Ninja — as in the story of the tortoise and the hare — since his runs tended to be slow and steady. He wasn't very fast at anything other than the climbing wall.

"Still, you should just go for it," Ty urged. "Push yourself, see how fast you can go. Who knows?"

Tara arrived just in time to hear him. "Don't listen to him, JJ," she advised. "Just go how you're comfortable, okay?"

"Sure," JJ said, but as he took his place on the start mat, he kept thinking about what Ty had said. Should he go for it? Throw caution to the wind, try to beat Benny's time?

"Whenever you're ready, ninja," the PA said.

JJ realized that his intro package had already finished and it was time to begin. He'd been so busy thinking about what Ty said that he'd forgotten to get nervous!

The nerves hit him as soon as he jumped onto the first balance step. He had never been particularly strong on balance obstacles, and he wobbled and almost fell immediately.

Picture yourself doing it perfectly, he thought, remembering what Noah had told him about overcoming stage fright. *And remember that you love this.*

He pushed off, somehow landing much better on the second step . . . and the third, fourth, fifth, and sixth ones, too. Soon he was on the mat, relieved to have survived Stepping Out.

Then he remembered that the timer was running. He

almost leaped forward immediately so he wouldn't lose even a second. But he shook his head and forced himself to wait, to catch his breath and his balance. He was going to do this his way — slow and steady.

He studied the setup for Monkey Business, ignoring the cheers and whistles from the crowd, making sure he knew exactly what he had to do. Then he jumped up and grabbed the first rope.

At the end of the obstacle, he was smiling. That had been fun!

I really do love doing this, he thought. *Okay, what's next?*

Bar None was a blast, even though it was hard and JJ's arm muscles were aching by the end. Touch and Go was even harder, and he almost knocked over the third vase. But it stayed upright, and he made it to the other side without getting eliminated. He'd been pretty good at the Loco Ladder, and today was no exception. He suspected he might even have made up some time on that one.

"Climb that Cliff! Climb that Cliff!" he chanted right along with the audience, glancing up to the top of the next obstacle.

He made it up easily, and then just barely made it through Round and Round by skipping across the balls as fast as he could so he didn't have time to lose his balance.

That will help with my time, too, he thought.

But he stayed slow and careful on Door to Door, which was a little tricky, just as Benny had warned him. He also took his time on the Funky Fishnet, which involved jumping from a trampoline onto a swing and then climbing across a rope ladder.

Before he knew it, there was only one obstacle left: the Wall Crawl. JJ stared up at it, wondering if the tired muscles in his arms and legs would hold out.

"Only one way to find out," he murmured.

He pressed his palms against the two smooth walls. Then he lifted his legs, jamming his feet onto the walls. Crawling like a spider, he inched his way up . . . up . . . up . . .

And then he was at the top! "He did it!" Mellie cried over the loudspeaker as the audience went wild. "JJ beat the course! Good going, JJ!"

JJ was so tired he could barely lift his arms in victory. But his smiling muscles felt just fine, and he grinned so widely he thought his face might split in two. Everyone was cheering and looking at him — and it felt great! Maybe it really was okay being special once in a while if it felt like this. Because he knew he'd earned it. He'd beaten the course, slow and steady.

"I did it!" he whispered.

Thirty-Four

"HE DID IT!" Izzy exclaimed, so proud of JJ she could burst. She glanced at the timer. "He won't beat Benny's time or Chen's, either. But he did it!"

"Yeah." Mackenzie was filming the whole thing with her phone. "That was amazing!"

"Come on, let's go meet him." Ty was already pushing his way through the throng of spectators.

By the time they reached JJ, his parents and sister were there, too, along with Tara and the Santiagos. For a few minutes everyone just danced around, hugging and babbling excitedly. Izzy was looking for her chance to move in and give JJ a hug when she felt her phone vibrate in her pocket. She pulled it out and saw that it was a text—from Jess!

Izzy gulped, almost tucking the phone back into her pocket right away. She didn't want anything to ruin this amazing moment. But she couldn't resist clicking to read the text. Normally Jess's texts were very short. But this one was pretty long:

> Hey Iz, I know your at the ninja thing, sorry to interrupt. But I feel bad about the other night. I know this ninja stuff is your new thing, guess I was just feeling a lil left out or whatev. It was dumb, OK? Sorry for being such a jerk about it . . . Anyway, the party wasn't much fun w/o u. I hope u have a blast ninja-ing today and totally slay your course!

Izzy's eyebrows shot up in surprise. Then she smiled, texting back quickly:

> No, it's OK, I get it. Maybe I was kinda ignoring u too – sorry!! But hey – u don't have to feel left out. How about u come to the gym when I get back and try out this ninja stuff for yourself? It's as much fun as parkour, I know u will love it!!

She sent the text, then held her breath, wondering how Jess would respond. She didn't have to wait long—within seconds, another text popped up from Jess.

Sounds like a plan. See u then.

Izzy grinned, feeling happier than ever. Jess was so cool, so tough—Izzy never would have guessed she could feel left out.

Okay, so maybe she could've handled it better and not been such a jerk about it, she thought. *But hey—I guess I could've noticed she was feeling left out and invited her to the gym earlier, too. Nobody's perfect, right?*

She tucked her phone away and finally saw her chance to duck in and give JJ a big hug.

"You were great," she told him, shouting into his ear so he could hear her over the noise of the crowd. "You were great!"

"Thanks." He laughed, hugging her back. "I couldn't have done it without all of you. I mean it!"

A few hours later, the results were in. Benny was the winner, with Chen second . . . and JJ had ended up in fourth place! He'd been one of only six ninjas to beat the course.

"That's amazing!" Mackenzie cried. "You're amazing, JJ! Happy dance!"

She started jumping around, waving her long arms and legs like a puppet. Ty joined in first, then JJ and Kevin. Finally Izzy laughed and started dancing, too.

"Is that what you guys call a happy dance?" Noah said, grinning as he watched. "You could use some new moves. Here—like this . . ."

He joined in, doing some funky steps and spins. Izzy smiled and imitated him, quickly picking up on the moves.

"Hey, you're pretty good," Noah told her. "Did anyone ever tell you you should be a dancer?"

"Sorry, no time," Izzy replied with a laugh. "I'm too busy being a ninja!"

Thirty-Five

MACK ATTACKS . . . . . .

MY BLOG ABOUT INTERESTING STUFF

By Mackenzie Clark, age 10½, nerdgirl extraordinaire! (← *that last word means fab!*)

Today: MACK ATTACKS . . . . . . ninjas and ratings and the future, oh my!!!

Can you believe the summer's over? I've already been back at school for over a week, and it's getting kind of chilly at night. But never mind that — I have much more interesting things to talk about than the weather! I'm sure my loyal readers are already wondering what I thought of last night's season finale of the very first season of *Junior Ninja Champion*.

Actually, scratch that — loyal readers will already know what I thought — that it was **FAAAAAAAAAAAAAAAB**!

Seriously though, it was super fun to see my teammates on TV (again). Wasn't JJ the coolest? He didn't let the pressure go to his head, just kept it slow and steady and totally dominated a super tough course. Amazing!

The ratings for the show were pretty amazing, too, by the way. The producers already announced that *JNC* will be back next season. Will yours truly try out again? Will the Fit Kidz ninja team stay together and go for it next summer? Stay tuned to find out . . .

😉

Q&A WITH NINJA ALLYSSA BEIRD

After many years practicing gymnastics and many months of hard work at ninja gyms, Allyssa Beird competed on seasons eight and nine of the TV show *American Ninja Warrior,* where she became the second woman ever to make it to stage two of the finals. She hopes she can inspire others to face their fears, overcome obstacles, and never give up. Allyssa lives in Massachusetts, where she teaches fifth grade and works on her ninja skills.

Q. How was returning for another season of *American Ninja Warrior* different than competing for the first time? Did you change anything about the way you trained and prepared?

A. For my first season on the show, more than anything, I was just so excited to be training in the gym and entering the ninja world. While I did okay that season, I definitely felt different coming back for a second season. I knew what to expect in terms of the filming and how the show works behind the scenes, so I was more focused on the actual run while I was on the course. I spent the time leading up to my second season training more for whole-body strength, rather than for specific obstacles, like I had done the first time. It seemed to be a great strategy, so I think I'll stick with that for now!

Q. Can you tell us about your experience with getting to the final round? How does it feel to be the second woman ever to reach stage two?

A. I remember getting past the Propeller Bar in the stage one finals and thinking, "Well, at least I made it past the obstacle I failed on last year!" Then I got through the next obstacle, and the next, and the next . . . before I realized it, I was standing before the final obstacle. It didn't quite feel real until I saw that 0:30, 0:29, 0:28 on the countdown clock as I was swinging through the Flying Squirrel. When I hit the buzzer, I felt both excitement and calm accomplishment. That was what I came to do!

It was bittersweet going to stage two without any other females. I fully expected to compete in the final round with at least one or two other strong women, but it was a pretty cool feeling being able to represent women, and myself, in stage two! I remember thinking about Jessie Graff, the first female to complete stage one, as I hit the stage one buzzer, and realizing I was also making a bit of my own history in that moment. Being only the second woman to reach stage two, I felt like I joined some sort of elite club. Hopefully that club will continue to grow as we all get stronger!

Q. What has life been like since competing on the show? Does anything feel different? What is it like to watch yourself on TV?

A. Since my last season on the show, life has been busy as ever! When I'm at school teaching, I'm Ms. Beird, just like I've always been. A lot of the students in my school will wave to me in the halls or smile excitedly, but other than that it's pretty normal. Outside of school, in the ninja world, there's definitely a bit more of a buzz. I've received so many messages through social media about being an inspiration to young girls and boys, aspiring athletes, and families who are inspired by my dual "teacher/ninja" life. Everyone is so supportive and wonderful! It feels different to have so many people looking up to me, because I still feel pretty normal: I'm just . . . me! This also made it a little weird to watch myself on TV my first season. I'm a bit more used to it now, and it's exciting to see what NBC decides to air, and I get to share in rewatching some exciting moments with family and friends. It's also been absolutely amazing to have something like *The Ellen [DeGeneres] Show* or the *Today* show reach out to me! I never dreamed I would do anything cool enough to get invited on *The Ellen Show,* so that was a very surreal experience. Most of the time, though, I wake up and continue my daily routine of being me!

Q. What does your pre-competition routine look like? Do you get nervous or have any last-minute rituals to stay calm and focused?

A. I love talking about this with other ninjas on the show. When I compete in local gym competitions, I get SO nervous! I feel like I'm out of breath before I begin, and I'll get shaky. However, unlike many other ninjas, when I walk up the steps to the starting platform of *American Ninja Warrior,* I usually feel calm and ready to go. I'll take a few deep breaths before starting, but once I'm on the course, I'm focused and working toward my goal of hitting that buzzer at the end. It's such a fun experience that I make sure to focus on that more than the pressure of competing.

I don't have any pre-run rituals, aside from visualizing the course. I'll run through the course in my head over and over again and try to imagine each obstacle in real time: what it feels like, how my body will move through the obstacles, how long it will take to finish each one, how to dismount. Visualizing is something I've had to really train myself to do, but it's a very helpful strategy to make a course I've never touched before seem familiar!

Q. How often do you train? Do you balance ninja workouts with other methods of exercise?

A. My training schedule is probably not as intense as most people would imagine. I train at ninja gyms Monday and Tuesday nights; I try to go rock climbing at a local rock climbing gym on Wednesday or Thursday; and Sunday, I do a leg-day workout of some kind. In between these scheduled workouts, I do a lot of pull-ups, squats, and leg work (things I can do in my living room), and I make sure to stretch and roll out my muscles with a foam roller. Rest days are just as important as workout days, so staying healthy and listening to your body is a must! Now that I'm more familiar with the obstacles, I use my ninja gym days as fun training days, and the in-between workouts as my strengthening days. Something I'd like to add to my training is more running, but it's been a hard thing to make time for in my busy schedule!

Q. Are there any obstacles that you feel like you've mastered? Any that still seem impossible?

A. It's hard to say that you've mastered an obstacle in the ninja world because someone will always find a way to give it a twist that will throw you off. That being said, I'm very comfortable on the Salmon Ladder, and I love working on the peg board! Once I found a technique on these two obstacles that worked for me, I was able to play around more and challenge myself in different ways. It's a great feeling to compare where I used to be, when I was unable to even complete one rung on the Salmon Ladder or one move on the peg board, to where I am now. I can move up, down, backwards, forward, skip rungs, complete rungs with a partner on the bar, and I'm even working on flipping between the rungs! These types of workouts beat the regular gym any day.

An obstacle I am forever struggling with is the Cliffhanger. Finger and grip strength are something that you need to continually train or else you lose it, and I have a hard time keeping up with it enough to feel really good on the Cliffhanger. While I don't see any obstacle as impossible, this one definitely doesn't make me feel excited to jump up and go. Hopefully I'll feel differently as I continue to work on it, but it's always good to have something with which to compare your strengths and something to work toward!

Q. What's your next ninja goal? How do you stay challenged?

A. My next goal is to beat stage two and be the first female to break through to stage three! I'm continually honing my training to work toward attaining that goal, and I know I will reach it! All good things take time, and if you're willing to put in that time and effort and work through the good days and the bad, you can reach all of your goals!

Every time I get into the ninja gym, there are new challenges. I train with a great group of ninjas and we're constantly challenging one another. We come up with fun courses and try to race through them. We also bring new life to the obstacles we already know by adding in a higher swing, a bigger reach, or a longer jump. Most challenges for me, however, are not found directly in the gym. Working full-time as a teacher, working for my dad's website business, finding some quiet relaxing time for myself, and still finding the time to train and make sure I'm listening to what my body needs (staying hydrated, taking a rest day, etc.) are sometimes bigger challenges than the most challenging obstacle in the gym! Setting little goals for myself helps me stay focused. If I was able to complete eight consecutive Salmon Ladder transfers, next time let's go for nine or ten! If you are constantly working toward your goals and feeling proud of your accomplishments and hard work, you will always find ways to continue to challenge yourself and set the bar higher and higher (literally and figuratively). It's a great feeling!

Q. What are your best tips for anyone working on their ninja skills or interested in trying?

A. If you're interested at all in trying out the ninja world, I would absolutely encourage you to do it! The one thing to know about entering this "ninja life" is that the moment you step into a ninja gym or decide you want to train as a ninja, you are welcomed into our ninja family for life. I started training at a ninja gym on a whim and knew nobody. Now, I can't imagine my life without these amazing people!

If you don't feel ready for a ninja gym quite yet, start with pull-ups. Not feeling a pull-up yet? See how long you can hang on a bar! Work on your grip strength, then slowly work up to holding yourself on the bar with bent arms (this is called a lock-off). If you have a resistance band, use this to help with pull-ups.

Balance and agility are also very important skills to train. Walk down the edge of sidewalks or concrete parking space barriers, leap across painted parking lot lines, and stride down the track. Becoming comfortable with moving your body will naturally translate to comfortableness on obstacles. Play on playgrounds and connect with your inner child! Find ways to work out that are fun and that you look forward to. You don't have to be a pro athlete to be a great ninja: all it takes is a little bit of time, some dedication, and a whole lot of heart! Catch you in the ninja gym!

To learn more about Allyssa and her ninja journey, visit allyssabeird.com.

ABOUT THE AUTHOR

CATHERINE HAPKA will never be mistaken for a ninja, but she has published more than two hundred books for kids in all age groups from board books to young adult novels. When she's not writing, Cathy enjoys horseback riding, animals of all kinds, reading, gardening, music, and travel. She lives in an old house on a small farm in Chester County, Pennsylvania, where she keeps three horses, a small flock of chickens, and too many cats.